A
Honeymoon
at
Seaside Cottage

Alexandra Wholey

Copyright

Dedication

For my family, thanks for all your support, with love always xx

A Note From The Author

If you have been here before, welcome back!

If you are new here, hello and welcome to my Scottish contemporary romance series, set in Mossbrae, in the Inner Hebrides. I hope you, like many of our residents, will fall in love and never want to leave!

This is a standalone series and can be read in any order.
For reference, this is the fourth book in the series.

1. A Year at Honeybee Cottage.
Eilidh Andersen returns to Mossbrae after a long absence, and having vowed not to fall in love, reunites with hunky farmer, Angus Kincaid, her childhood friend. (Eilidh's POV)

2. Christmas at Honeybee Cottage.
Christmas has come to Mossbrae... Wedding planning is in the air! (Eilidh's POV)

3. A Summer Wedding in the Highlands.
Eilidh and Angus are finally tying the knot! Get ready for the wedding of the year! (Grace's POV)

Let me reintroduce you to the residents of Mossbrae:

The Main Players

Eilidh Kincaid (nee Andersen) Our heroine beekeeper, owns and runs Cairnmhor Honey, and married to Angus.

Angus Kincaid Fourth generation sheep and deer farmer. Lives at Honeybee Cottage with wife Eilidh, and runs honey business, Cairnmhor Honey. Also runs family farm, Cairnmhor Farm, a two hundred acre hill farm, with two hundred Blackface Sheep and fifty Red Deer.

Joe Kincaid Patriarch of the Kincaid family, widower of Annabelle, father to Grace, Angus and Robyn. Used to run Cairnmhor Farm until ill health meant early retirement. Now lives on the farm with Grace and her family.

Grace Wallace (nee Kincaid) Angus's older sister, married to Paul, and mother of Ollie and Mhairi. Lives at Cairnmhor Farm where she is carer to her elderly father, Joe. Runs Four Ducks Bakery near the harbour. Rents out Duck Cottage.

Paul Wallace Married to Grace and father of Ollie and Mhairi. Helps Angus to run Cairnmhor Farm.

Mhairi and Ollie Grace and Paul's kids who help out on the farm and love beekeeping. Also own Runner Ducks.

Robyn Gillan (nee Kincaid) Local vet. Younger sister of Grace and Angus. Married to Orion. Currently pregnant with her rainbow baby.

Orion Gillan Local vet. Married to Robyn.

Enid, Maudie and Nelly. (The Trinity) Triplet elderly spinster godmothers to the Kincaid siblings. Love a good gossip and matchmaking, and are responsible for Angus and Eilidh getting together. Always on the look out for another chance to matchmake.

Side Characters and Animals

(Appear in Book 1:)

Aggie Gillan: Orion's mother

Ava Gillan: Robyn's sister-in-law

Peter Gillan: Robyn's brother-in-law

Nigel Landlord of The Dog and Duck pub in Mossbrae. Dating Maudie.

Dash and Dram Angus and (later) Eilidh's border collies.

Waffle Aggie's cat.

Strawberry, Apple, Custard and Jelly Ollie and Mhairi's Runner Ducks.

(Appear in Books 2 and 3)

Rory Gordon Joe Kincaid's nephew and the Kincaid sibling's cousin. Owns and runs an estate, Capercaillie in Fochabers, which is the venue for Angus and Eilidh's wedding. Married to Isla and father to William.

Isla Gordon Rory's wife and mother to William.

William Gordon Rory and Isla's son.

Rhona Rory and Isla's house keeper. Grandmother of Jo and Leanna McKinnon.

Achie Lennox Grace's ex-boyfriend whom she was at catering college with but who is out for revenge. **(Appears only in Book 3)**

(Appear in Books 3 and 4:)

Leanna McKinnon Twin sister of Jo, wants to be a chef, and at the end of Book 3, moves to Mossbrae to work with Grace at the Four Ducks Bakery.

Jo McKinnon Twin sister of Leanna, granddaughter of Rhona and niece of Alice and Ray. Lives in Braerannoch. Has just graduated vet school.

Dougie Sinclair Son of family friend, Jim. Has moved to Mossbrae to help Angus on the farm. The next matchmaking candidate according to the locals.

Alice McKinnon Aunt of Leanna and Jo. Lives at Elderflower Farm with her husband Ray. Loves farming, cooking and beekeeping. Owner of Seaside Cottage.

Ray McKinnon Uncle of Leanna and Jo. Lives and runs Elderflower farm with his wife Alice. Owner of Seaside Cottage.

Brock Ray's border collie.

Marigold a menace of a sheep.

Glossary

Aye Yes

Baltic. Very cold (usually winter related)

Bairns Children

Blethering Bickering

Braw Good/ Really good

Cannae Can't

Ceilidh Traditional Scottish party with music and dancing.

Clype. A gossip/ Tell tale

Couldnae. Couldn't

Craic Enjoyable social activity, a good time.

Didnae. Didn't

Dinnae. Don't

Doesnae. Doesn't

Dreich. Rainy dull weather

Hadnae. Hadn't

Hasnae. Hasn't

Havenae. Haven't

Hen. Term of endearment towards a lady

Isnae. Is not/ Isn't

Och. Oh! An exclamation of expression

Sláinte Cheers

Shouldnae shouldn't

Shouldae Should have

Sleekit. Sly, cunning

Stoating.   It's stoating down, rain falling so hard it bounces off the ground.

Stooshie. To bicker or have a quarrel

Stramash. To have a full blown argument.

Wasnae Wasn't

Weans. Another term for Children

Willnae Will Not

Whisht   To shush someone

Wouldnae Wouldn't

A
Honeymoon
at
Seaside Cottage

Alexandra Wholey

Content Warning

*T*his page is the page for you if you want to know what potentially difficult content you might encounter in this book. This may contain SPOILERS which hint at plot lines (or even briefly moments in the story.)

Death of relative (grandmother, off page) discussed and mentioned briefly on page.

On page discussion of ectopic pregnancy of secondary character resulting in baby loss (before 12 weeks) and coping with this loss is a theme in the story.

Destruction of beehives and death of bees, mentioned briefly in conversation.

Prologue

raerannoch
Outer Hebrides

The waves crashed against the harbour sea wall as Jo McKinnon, and her twin sister, Leanna, breathing in the salty sea air as they together walked along the shingle beach.

"Och, I miss it here. Mossbrae is just like it," Leanna sighed with happiness, blonde hair whipping around her face before she caught it and fastened it into a plait.

"Are you enjoying the job?" Jo asked.

"Aye, Grace is a lovely boss. She's so kind hearted and hard working."

"Those honey cakes you brought home with you are amazing."

"They're home made with Cairnmhor honey. Remember, the honey business Eilidh and Angus run, the one I was telling you about?"

"Aye, Aunty Alice has been on about getting some hives. She wants to start beekeeping."

"That's fantastic!" Leanna exclaimed, adding with a playful nudge. "She can start making her own honey cakes. I'll give her the recipe Grace uses."

"That's a great idea."

They glanced up the cliff path to the white stone farm at the top. Elderflower Farm had been in the McKinnon family for three generations and was now in their aunt and uncle's possession.

"They'll have a lot to take on, getting hives on top of the Shetlands, and the Valais Blacknose sheep," Jo said, crossing her arms against a sudden blast of icy wind.

Leanna laughed. "I know. It's all Aunty Alice's idea. She was inspired after she had been talking to Gran who told her all about Cairnmhor Honey. You know, you should come to Mossbrae."

Leanna turned to her now, as they paused, watching seals bobbing in the harbour. "It'll be lovely to see you and spend some time together."

Jo glanced at her twin now, and shook her head. "I've only just started my placement here. I cannae start asking for time off and I'm working all hours, including weekends."

"I know. And plus there's Colin to consider..." Leanna teased, and Jo felt the blush spread across her face at the mention of her longterm boyfriend.

"Ah, look at the look on your face. If that's not a look of true love, I dinnae know what is. When's there going to be a wedding?"

Jo's eyes shone with happiness, tucking a strand behind her ear. "Och, you'd have to ask him about that... He's been very secretive on the matter."

"As long as you ask me to be your maid of honour, I dinnae care," Leanne chuckled, threading her arm through

4

hers as she glanced across at the harbour. "I'd better go and pack. I've to get the ferry back to Mossbrae soon."

The wind had calmed once Leanna made it to the ferry. Alice and Jo had gone with her to see her off.

"It's been lovely to see you. I love you being able to come back and see us. We miss you when you're not here," Alice murmured as she pulled Leanna into a tight hug.

"I miss Braerannoch too, it's such a lovely place. Mossbrae is so like it, it's like a home from home. I'm no' able to come back for a few weeks, we're really busy at the bakery."

Jo pulled her into a hug. "I shall come and see you. I'll try and get a free weekend."

"Aye. You need to keep me posted on any news with you and Colin!"

"What news?" Alice asked, glancing between her nieces with barely concealed excitement. "Have I missed something?"

"Och, I would think they'll be some happy news soon enough...you'd better buy a hat," Leanna smiled, meeting Jo's gaze mischievously.

"Wait and see!" Jo laughed as Leanna dragged her wheelie case down the ramp and onto the ferry, waving goodbye as she went.

Chapter One

*M*ossbrae.
Three Months Later.

At Four Ducks Bakery, beekeeper Eilidh Kincaid carried the pallet of jars containing freshly made blackberry honey into the shop.

"Here we go, is that enough to do your latest batch?"

"Aye, that's grand," Grace, her sister-in-law nodded enthusiastically as she helped her take the jars into the back. "The customers are gonnae be falling over themselves to get their hands on this next batch! How much do I owe you?"

"Och, pay me back in honey cakes. Speaking of which, something smells delicious!" Eilidh added.

"Aye, Leanna is just icing up the latest batch of orange blossom cupcakes."

"They've turned out fantastic," Leanna added, her face bright with happiness. "Jo loved them last time I took some home."

"Keep one for her today as a welcome to Mossbrae. What time is she arriving?" Grace asked. Jo was arriving to collect some nucs for her aunt Alice and was planning to stay in

Mossbrae for the weekend. Nucs were the shortened name for of a nucleus colony, a small sized hive in which you kept a small colony of bees. Nucs were used when splitting a hive, and when introducing a new colony to a new hive.

"The ferry should be here any minute now," Eilidh replied, glancing down at the harbour, at the waves crashing against the harbour sea wall. Outside, it was a bright summer's day, with a brisk breeze coming in from the sea. In the far distance, they could see the ferry heading towards the harbour, over from the mainland with the next batch of tourists ready to explore the village and it's beautiful surrounding beach and further into Mossbrae, the rugged glens beyond.

"Hey, just think," Grace nudged Eilidh, barely able to conceal her own excitement. "Next weekend, it'll be you and Angus heading off on the ferry. A whole week in Paris! Now that's what I call a honeymoon!"

"I cannae believe it either!" Eilidh beamed back. "I've only just got Angus to get the cases down from the loft!"

"Och, you only need a suitcase, your passport and your credit card!" Grace assured her.

"I love Paris! It's so romantic!" Leanna sighed as she stacked the cupcakes behind the counter. I hear you can get to eat in the Michelin star restaurant at the top of the Eiffel Tower..."

"Aye? Get Angus to book a table!" Grace chipped in.

"Dinnae fret, I definitely will!" Eilidh nodded.

. . .

They turned at the sight of the ferry docking in the harbour and the passengers alighting. Amongst the raincoat wearing, bobble hat wearing tourists with their maps and hiking boots, was a tall, elegantly featured brunette, dressed in jeans and a red T shirt and boots, despite the summer heat, pulling a navy wheelie case. When she spotted the bakery and saw the three women waving through the front window, her face broke into a grin and she quickened her pace.

"Hello!" Leanna rushed forward and enveloped Jo in a hug. "Welcome to Mossbrae!"

She turned to Grace and Eilidh and introduced them.

"How was the journey?" Grace asked.

"It was pleasant enough," Jo said. "I feel a wee bit wobbly though. I dinnae have strong sea legs."

"Aye, it's a wee bit choppy today. I'll get you a brew," Grace said and headed into the back.

"Have an orange blossom honey cupcake too, they're freshly made. With Cairnmhor honey," Leanna added.

"Thanks. Aye, I'm looking forward to seeing how Aunt Alice gets on with her new nucs. She's really excited to get started." Jo said, and took a seat on a chair behind the counter.

"I'm glad to hear it. If she needs any help or advice tell her to give us a call. Or there's my friend, Buzz. He's an inspector and he travels around here and further out Braerannoch way."

"Is that his real name?" Jo asked, with a light frown.

"Aye," Eilidh replied. "I bet his parents didnae think he'd work with bees when they named him. I think they named him after Buzz Aldrin."

"Ah."

She glanced around, admiring the bakery as Grace brought in the tea.

"I love it in here, it's so light and airy," Jo said, as she took a sip of tea.

"I love it at the gloaming time, when the light is fading across the harbour and all the street lights are reflected in the water," Grace replied with a warm smile.

"And at Christmas," Eilidh added. "Walking on the beach in the moonlight on a crisp winter's day is lovely."

"Reminds me of Braerannoch," Leanna and Jo said in unison, grinning.

"Speaking of which," Leanna piped up. "How did it go with Colin?"

Jo looked awkward. "We broke up."

"Wait, what?" Leanna cried. "You never said anything…"

"I knew you were busy here and I didnae want to upset you. It's alright, work is helping me take my mind off him."

Her blue eyes were serious, and Leanna felt her heart sink.

"What happened? It's been three months…"

"He moved to New Zealand…"

She recalled the events of that night. It had been a busy Friday night at The Thistle, and Jo had sat, feeling her heart racing, waiting for Colin to arrive. He'd told her he had a surprise but that's all she knew and the thought made her feel a mix of panic and excitement.

"You look gorgeous," Colin said, with a low whistle as she glanced up and saw him walking towards their table. Her heart gave a leap. Oh no, he was wearing his favourite blue pinstriped shirt, and and suit trousers. This was going to be serious surprise…

"Are you alright? You look on edge."

Jo had given herself a mental shake and nodded. "Aye, I'm fine. You scrub up well too!"

Colin had smiled back as he sat down. With his tousled blond hair and grey-blue eyes, he reminded her of actor Johnny Flynn, and she was transported back to the first day they had met at school, lining up to do their Highers. "Shall we order some champagne?"

"Champagne? Do they even sell champagne here?"

"Aye, of course they do. I've spoken to Ursula. She said they even have Moët."

"Really?" Jo had gasped in surprise. "Och, I never knew that. So, what do you fancy?"

"Besides you?" Colin asked, with a smirk.

Jo had felt the blush creep up her cheeks, and had to look away as he held her gaze, glancing down instead at her outfit. She was wearing her favourite peacock blue dress, matching shoes and feather earrings.

"Ursula was saying it's seafood special night. So what do you fancy? Prawn and chive risotto? I know you love risotto."

"Aye, it sounds nice," Jo said absently, as she checked the menu. For some reason, she felt nervous, and agitated, with a gut feeling something didn't feel right.

"Think I'll have steak and chips," Colin replied brightly.

"For seafood special night?"

"Aye, why not? I'll go and order…"

Then, he had stood, and gone to the bar to order.

As she watched him, she thought about Leanna's jokes about him proposing, and she felt a thrill of excitement at the possibility.

. . .

"Well, that's the orders made," Colin had announced on his return, and slid into his chair. "Are you sure you're alright?"

Jo nodded, her mind lingering on Leanna's words. "I'm wondering about this surprise of yours."

"I was gonnae tell you after pudding. How was work?"

"It's been really busy at work. I cannae wait to get onto my placement. It's gonnae be such a good experience."

"Two chowders for start," Ursula had announced as she brought over the champagne and their starters.

Jo thanked her and took a sip. It was creamy, thick, and lightly seasoned. There were even chunks of white fish in the broth, which were sweet and lightly flavoured.

"This is braw," Jo had murmured, feeling herself relax as she enjoyed her food.

"Wait until you try the risotto!" Colin had added with a wink.

He was right, she had to admit as he poured her a glass of champagne which was fizzy and sharp on her tongue. The risotto when it came was prawn, chives and peas, and was absolutely delicious. There was also a sharp undertone of white wine and she almost sighed with pleasure.

"I'll have to get the recipe from Ursula," Jo had exclaimed as she spooned the last spoon into her mouth, realising she'd been so lost in enjoying her food, she'd eaten in almost complete silence.

"Shall we get the puddings?" She had asked, dabbing her mouth with a napkin, feeling calmer now, thanks to the champagne and the delicious food. "The strawberry cranachan looks nice…"

He cleared his throat. "Aye, that's grand. Jo, I wanted to talk to you…"

"Aye?"

Jo had straightened, focusing her gaze on him seriously, bracing herself for him to get the ring box out of his pocket. Marriage was something she had always wanted, but it still felt a bit sudden, and she'd wanted a proposal somewhere memorable like Arthur's Seat… somewhere a little bit more romantic…not necessarily in their local pub which was so busy, they could barely hear each other speak.

Colin had cleared his throat as he leant forward and grasped her hands in his.

"Jo, I have some exciting news."

She had felt a surge of nerves, her heart racing.

"You know I've always wanted to run my own farm, and well, I've finally found somewhere. It's in New Zealand."

"New Zealand?! That's wonderful!" Jo had cried with joy. "I'm so happy for you. You kept that quiet…"

"I didnae want to get your hopes up," Colin had replied awkwardly.

"What?" Jo laughed, and had glanced up at him to see the seriousness in his eyes. "Why not?"

"That's the thing. I'm moving next week."

Jo's eyes widened. "Next week? That's quick!"

"Aye, I know. But it's perfect. And that's the thing. I know everything we know is here, our jobs, our life, our families… But I'm ready to make the step towards the future. I think it lies in New Zealand. Jo…"

He took her hand, and she felt her stomach begin to churn with nerves.

She grabbed her champagne flute, and took a long sip to calm her nerves, as he continued, oblivious.

"We've been together for such a long time…and you're one of the most wonderful women I know. I'm so happy we met, and you've been part of my life for so long.."

Oh, he *was* going to propose!

Jo's mind raced. There was so much to organise. She'd have to give at least a month's notice at work, and there was the lease on the flat, and then there was Aunty Alice and Uncle Ray to consider…

"I know your life is here. Everything you know is here. But I want more than that, and that's the thing. I've been thinking about it for a long time, and I'm so sorry, but I dinnae see a future for us. I'm moving to New Zealand on my own…"

"Wow!" Leanna gasped as Jo awkwardly finished her tea.

"Och, I'm sorry to hear that," Grace murmured.

"Hey, how about we head to the cottage, and I show you around the hives?" Eilidh suggested, wanting to ease the awkwardness, as she exchanged a glance with Grace who nodded in silent agreement.

"That sounds perfect." Jo agreed. "I'm keen to learn a bit about beekeeping."

"Och, wait, here are the keys to Duck Cottage," Leanna added, handing over her door keys. For the time being, she was renting Grace's old cottage, Duck Cottage, on the other side of Mossbrae. "Just let yourself in and make yourself at home."

"Thanks. I'll see you tonight."

And with that, they headed off.

They reached Honeybee Cottage twenty minutes later, and when Jo got out, breathing in the heady scent of roses, honeysuckle and jasmine as she followed Eilidh in through the wooden gate.

"This is beautiful!" she exclaimed, admiring the peach climbing roses above the door as Eilidh let them in round the side of the house and into the back garden.

"The nucs are in the back garden, along with the rest of the hives, and the extraction shed. I'll give you a tour."

Eilidh pushed the gate open to reveal a small but lovely back garden, surrounded by a red brick wall. In the centre stood a tall white Buddleia tree, in full bloom and covered with honeybees and butterflies, and along the borders were roses, and peonies. In the far corner was a large shed and along the back wall were six bee hives.

"This is lovely," Jo enthused, admiring the hives. The air was filled with birdsong and the gentle hum of the bees. "I'd love to have a garden like this back home one day."

"I inherited the cottage from my late grandmother," Eilidh beamed. "We used to have beekeeping lessons here when I was a child."

"That must have been wonderful."

"It was," she replied. "She taught me all I know."

"It's lovely to have have had such a close relationship. I don't get to see Gran as much as I'd like but one day, I'd love to live near her."

"How is she getting on with Cedric now?" Eilidh asked.

"They're getting on really well," Jo said, her face breaking into a warm smile. "It's like young love."

"I bet," Eilidh said as she reached for her beesuit. "Right, let's get suited up and I'll show you the hives."

She went into the honey shed and got a spare suit. Jo pulled it on, and Eilidh lit the smoker.

"We light the smoker to calm the bees," she explained, as she wafted it across the hive.

Jo nodded as she opened the hive, which filled the air with the hum of bees. "On top, we have the honey supers where the honey is held. This has been a productive year so we've had to put two on each hive. The honey is stored on these frames here, hidden with beeswax here."

She pointed at the wax on the frames. "The pollen is stored and turned into honey here. Can you see the sheen on the honey, here?"

Jo nodded. "Does the colour change with the sort of pollen used?"

"Aye, it does," Eilidh replied. "Dandelion pollen is orange, and apple pollen is yellow. Blackberry is an almost khaki colour, honeysuckle, dark yellow, and pollen from roses is lighter yellow."

"That's fantastic," Jo replied. "I'll have to let Aunty Alice know once she starts getting honey."

"Aye, it doesnae take too long to start getting honey," Eilidh replied. "It takes about two seasons usually."

She checked another frame. "These frames look full of honey, which is brilliant for the middle of the season."

"What about infections?" Jo asked. "Do honeybees get ill?"

Eilidh nodded. "Aye, there's varroa mites, and foulbrood. For varroa mites, you can buy powders to feed the bees. Bees with varroa mites aren't healthy, they are weak and won't produce a good honey crop."

"What about foulbrood?"

"Och, foulbrood is a nasty infection which affects the larvae," Eilidh began when there was a beep of a car horn.

"Hello!"

Robyn, Eilidh's other sister-in-law waved as she walked in through the back gate. Dressed in a purple floral maternity dress, blonde hair fluffy around her shoulders, she was glowing with happiness.

"Hello!" Eilidh called, delighted, her gaze fell to her pregnant belly."What brings you here? You look glowing!"

Robyn beamed. "I'm not too bad. I've felt a wee bit sick, and I'm constantly hungry, but I cannot not be grateful. I cannae believe in five months, Baby will be here. I'm craving some orange blossom honey. Have you got any spare? Dinnae fret, the doctor says I'm allowed."

"Aye, we've a few spare jars in the shed," Eilidh grinned. "I'll give you the keys and you go and help yourself. Had a busy morning?"

"Aye, I've been in the vet surgery all morning. I'm gonnae have to be careful near livestock now I'm pregnant, with illness and accidents, so I'll be doing less farm visits.."

"Jo knows what you mean," Eilidh replied. "Jo, this is my sister in law. Robyn, this is Jo, Leanna's sister. She's a vet graduate."

"Ah, that's grand. Are you enjoying it?"

"Aye, I love it," Jo replied. "I'm at my local practice back in Braerannoch. I'm moving onto livestock in the next few months."

"It's full of variation. I'm gonnae miss it once I go on maternity leave."

"Aye? When are you going on maternity leave?" Jo asked.

"Around Christmas," Robyn replied, and exchanged a

glance with Eilidh. "Actually, I'm looking for cover. Would you be interested?"

"It would be a good reason to stay," Eilidh added encouragingly.

"I'd have to think about it, I've only just started my placement," Jo replied with a brief hesitation. "Actually, Eilidh, could I buy some of that delicious orange blossom honey from you? Aunty Alice loved it last time Leanna brought some home."

"Och, head into the shed and help yourself," Eilidh replied.

"Are you sure?"

"Of course, go right ahead," she replied.

"Thanks, that's really kind of you," Jo replied, and headed off towards the shed.

"How are you going to persuade her to stay in Mossbrae?" Robyn asked, watching her. "Another matchmaking scheme?"

"Maybe..." Eilidh said with a glint of mischief in her eyes. "I worked for me and Angus."

"Aye?"

"Well, she's split up with her boyfriend and is clearly nursing a broken heart. Why don't we give her a reason to stay a little longer in Mossbrae and find someone to help her heal?"

"Are you talking about Dougie?"

"Aye, why not? He's young, and handsome. He's single from what I can gather. He doesnae spend every night down the pub drinking away his wages, and he loves animals."

"I think it sounds like a plan!" Robyn grinned. "Och, I do

love a bit of matchmaking. Like you said, it worked for you and Angus."

"Aye," Eilidh grinned, glancing down at her wedding ring. "It did."

"And next weekend you're off on honeymoon!" Robyn sighed. "It's so romantic. I wish I was off to Paris."

"You could have a baby moon, you know, a holiday afore baby arrives."

"Aye. That'd be a grand idea. So, how about you and Angus? Can we expect a honeymoon baby?"

"Och, you sound like Grace," Eilidh chuckled. "But to be honest, I dinnae think we've timed it right for a honeymoon baby."

"Are you trying?" Robyn asked in delight. "You never said anything!"

"I didnae want to upset you," Eilidh admitted, feeling slightly awkward. Robyn and her husband, Orion, had lost a baby when she had suffered an ectopic pregnancy resulting in emergency surgery, where she had almost also lost her life. This baby was her miracle baby, and Eilidh hadn't wanted to upset her further

"Och, dinnae be silly!" Robyn chided. "We need to look to the future, remember?" She stroked her belly, gazing at it fondly.

"So are you?" She promoted.

Eilidh nodded. "Well, I suppose we are, aye. We're just seeing how it goes...Got to enjoy the honeymoon first though!"

They turned to see Jo coming out of the honey shed with the jars of honey.

"It's an impressive set up you have in there. I see you have a Lyson honey extractor."

"Aye, Angus put up the honey shed for me when I first moved back," Eilidh replied. "I was just saying to Robyn, we should head to the farm, and show you around the sheep and deer. Get you some practice afore you start working with livestock back home."

"Thank you, that'd be grand," Jo beamed. "Thank you for showing me the hives."

"We'll take my car," Robyn suggested and closing the hives, and changing out of the bee suits, Eilidh and Jo followed her.

As they climbed into the car, Eilidh and Robyn exchanged a glance, knowing this little scheme was bound to pay off…

Chapter Two

*a*t Cairnmhor Farm, the hot summer air was filled with birdsong and the distant bleat of lambs up the hillside, as well as the buzz of the electric shears.

"Angus shears our own sheep instead of hiring it out," Eilidh explained as they pulled up in the farm yard, from where they could see Angus, Paul and Dougie over in the lower paddock ahead.

"Impressive," Jo said, as they walked over to the paddock. She glanced at the men, admiring in particular as Dougie grabbed the next ewe, and expertly ran the clippers across the fleece. As he held the ewe across his chest, leaning her against his knees, expertly moving the clippers down across the fleece, not leaving any nicks or tramlines. He's good at this, she thought, watching him. As she did so, her gaze trailed across his muscular forearms, he must be strong to be able to hold this ewe without any issues, she thought.

"That's Dougie," Eilidh's voice cut into her thoughts as she noticed her staring over. "He's helping us since the lambing season."

Jo nodded silently, but Eilidh was glad to see that she seemed to be lost in thought, her gaze fixed on him. Yes, she thought to herself, they would make a great couple.

"You know, I think we could all do with a drink, with all this hard work. It's hot, thirsty work," Grace added, pointedly.

Eilidh nodded in agreement, glancing across at Angus now, as he finished shearing another ewe. Her gaze trailed across his muscular forearms, and felt her stomach flutter with longing.

"Eilidh?"

She started, turning to Grace. "I was saying, we should take the lemonade over to the lads, aye?"

"Aye, we should. I'll give you a hand," she said as she watched as the ewe ran off to join the others, and Angus pass the heavy fleece to Paul, Mhairi and Ollie and helped them load it into a large jute bag, ready to be loaded onto the trailer and taken to market.

"Hullo," Angus called, as the three women made their way over with the cool boxes. "Are we glad to see that cool box! Dougie's suffering, eh?"

Dougie swiped his arm across his brow and nodded.

Eilidh handed him a bottle as she introduced Jo to everyone.

"Pleased to meet you," Jo said, taking a bottle to Dougie.

"Thanks," he said, as he let the freshly shorn ewe go. Jo noticed as he wiped his brow, he had eyes the colour of the finest whiskey, a rich amber, with long eyelashes. She took in his face, open and broad features, and felt a flicker of attraction in the pit of her stomach. "Thank you."

His face broke into a smile.

"Fancy giving shearing a try?" Angus asked Eilidh with a grin.

"Och, no!" Eilidh laughed. "I think I'll stick to the bees! Jo might like to have a try though, eh?"

Dougie offered the clippers to Jo. "I can hold the ewe whilst you have a turn, if you like?"

Jo shook her head, laughing. "Och, no, I dinnae want the ewe to be embarrassed. I had a turn at my uncle's farm once and the ewe ended up with a mohawk when I was done."

Dougie burst out laughing and Jo felt her heart race a little faster with that flicker of attraction between them.

"So are you staying in Mossbrae long?" Dougie asked.

"I'm just here for the weekend, staying with Leanna at Duck Cottgae. I'm here to collect the nucs from Eilidh for my aunty, who wants to start beekeeping."

"Well, Mossbrae is a lovely place to spend the weekend," Dougie replied. "Great scenery, and wildlife. The Dog and Duck pub does great food too."

"Aye, Leanna was telling me. I'm keen to explore the village. When I arrived, it reminds me so much of my home village, Braerannoch."

"Aye, it must be a braw place."

Jo nodded proudly. "It's lovely. It's out in the Outer Hebrides."

"I'll have to check it out when I get a day off next," Dougie grinned.

"They're getting on well," Grace whispered to Eilidh conspiratorially.

"Aye," Eilidh agreed. "I can see the sparks flying from here!"

"Are you two up to some matchmaking again?" Angus asked, catching the glance between them.

"Dougie's single, aye?" Eilidh asked him.

"Aye. I heard he's quite the catch down the village, according to The Trinity..." Angus replied. "Last time we were there for a drink he got chatted up quite a bit."

"Really?" Eilidh asked excitedly. "So is he looking for a girlfriend?"

Angus shrugged. "He's not said he isn't, and he and Jo seem to be getting on well though. Shame he's leaving afore Christmas."

"What? He's leaving?" Eilidh looked horrified.

"He's helping his family out back home for a couple of months."

"We have to get our plan in motion!" Eilidh gasped, exchanging a look with Grace.

"Och, dinnae fret, I'll work my magic whilst you head off on honeymoon."

"Thank you."

Turning to Angus now, she added. "I'm gonnae head back to the cottage to check the hives afore we start packing for the honeymoon."

"Och, you'll soon be on a plane, sipping champagne, and the farm will be a distant memory..." Grace added.

"Are you gonnae be alright running everything for the whole week? With the bees too?" Eilidh asked anxiously.

"Och, the bees will be fine," said Grace. "The kids can give me some pointers. Plus, Paul and Da will be around, and Wee Dougie will be here."

"'Wee Dougie'!" Eilidh laughed, and they glanced across at him and Jo now. "Dougie's nearly thirty!"

"Aye, and he's of marriageable age according to you…" Angus chuckled.

"Well, it worked for us!" Eilidh cried.

"Eventually! Only took twenty years to get you together!" Grace cut in.

"You forget I'd sworn off men!" Eilidh protested, laughing.

"Until that summer I help you paint the cottage," Angus winked at her as he took a long sip of his drink, reminding Eilidh of that summer they had got together. Her gaze trailed across his muscular forearms, and she felt her stomach flutter at the sight of him. He met her gaze and gave her a wink, as though he could read her mind.

"And now you're married…" Grace gave a soft chuckle and put an arm around her shoulders.

"Sure you dinnae fancy a go, Paddington?" Angus asked, gesturing to the electric shears. "We'll make a shepherdess out of you, yet…"

"Well, I do have a sheepdog, but I couldnae cope with shearing in this heat!" Eilidh replied, wiping beads of sweat from her own forehead as Angus offered her his drink. She took a long sip, and it was sharp, tangy and delicious.

"That lemonade is braw!" She smiled. "Right, I'm gonnae head off. I'll see you back at the cottage."

"See you in a bit," Angus said, smiling at her. "Do you need a lift?"

Eilidh shook her head. "It's a gorgeous day, I'll walk."

"See you later then."

They grinned at each other, and Eilidh turned, watching Dougie and Jo laughing as they shared a joke.

"Dougie, why don't you show Jo around the farm? She's a vet graduate and she's gonnae be working with livestock."

"Aye, of course. We can head up and see the deer after this if you like?"

Jo nodded. "That sounds grand."

"And so it begins…" Grace grinned, patting Eilidh on the shoulder as she headed off back to Honeybee Cottage.

The hot summer sun was beating down when Eilidh reached Honeybee Cottage and pulled on her bee suit, grabbing the smoker, ready to continue her check with the hives before she had to start packing.

She hesitated, hit by a wave of nostalgia and grief for past memories here with her late grandmother, Marianne, of her beekeeping lessons, and she was saddened that she wasn't here to see how successful she had become. She glanced across at the six hives now, thinking about Cairnmhor Honey, and how proud Marianne would have been. She closed her eyes, loving the warmth of the sun on her face, hearing the birdsong high above her, and the hum of bees flying around, visiting the flowers. Taking a deep breath, enjoying the heady scent of Buddleia and roses.

Eilidh wafted the smoker over the hive, and opened the lid, and indulged in the soothing sound of the bees humming as she lifted the frame and inspected it. Her heart raced a little quicker with excitement, seeing the honey filling the frame. This season had been a success, and she was especially pleased to see the different shades, indicating the variety of plants and flowers the bees had collected pollen from. This season was going to produce even more variety.

Replacing the frame, she checked another, pleased to see that it was also filled with honey. Then she replaced it, and checked another frame. That too, was full. Wow, this honey season was going to be one of the best yet...

She checked the brood box too, and the first three frames were fine, filled with eggs and stored pollen, full of bees, and Eilidh felt her good mood increase.

But then, she got to the fourth frame, and her heart sank. She spotted it, a tiny black speck on the centre of the frame, spreading across the cells. She knew what it was immediately, and her blood ran cold.

"Och, no," she murmured, and reached for the next one. Again, she saw black specks spread across the frame where the eggs should be. She checked the remaining frames and found them to be clear, but that didn't mean the whole hive wasn't infected...

"Please don't let it be..." she murmured, shaking her head and feeling a sense of dread. "Not foulbrood..."

Foulbrood was a bacterial virus, with the potential to wipe out entire bee colonies. It was not infectious for people but for bees it was a killer. There were two varieties, European foulbrood, and American foulbrood, which was worse and highly contagious. She glanced across at the other hives, hoping she wasn't too late and that it had already spread.

Only one way to find out, she thought, heading inside to wash her hands before checking the rest of the hives. To her relief it appeared to be the only hive that was affected, and she felt a glimmer of relief. But the hive she was inspecting was her best hive. This year, it had had to have three honey supers, the most she had had this season, and she felt crushed she might have to destroy it.

Heading back inside, Eilidh changed, thinking about what to do next. When evidence of foulbrood was found, the first call should be to the bee inspector and report the problem so that any other hives in the area could be checked.

"Hello, Buzz, it's Eilidh," Eilidh said, voice trembling, making the call she had never thought she had had to make in all her career, a growing sense of dread and fear for the future of Cairnmhor Honey. If it turned out to be American Foulbrood, they could lose the business. She said a silent prayer in her head, mentally crossing all her fingers and toes, like a little child, and hoping, desperately hoping, it wasn't...

"Are you able to come over to Honeybee Cottage? I've found evidence of foulbrood..."

Chapter Three

"It's a good job I was in the area," Buzz said grimly when he arrived an hour later, already suited up, ready to make the inspection.

"Thank you for being able to come over so quickly," Eilidh said. "We're heading off on honeymoon this weekend, and I wanted to check the hives afore we go away…"

"You did the right thing. You need to report any evidence of foul brood by law," Buzz replied. He was a stocky man in his early fifties, bald and called as he said it 'a spade a spade.' "It's like TB in cattle…Right, we're gonnae check the hives again, and then assess if it is foulbrood."

He opened the hive and lifted a frame. "Well, you were right, it is foul brood… All we need to do is work out which one…"

He studied the frame, "The larvae are brown here, and across the frame… Can you see, here? There's evidence of a pepper pot brood pattern where the queen doesnae lay in all of the cells. The caps on the sealed cells are also uneven and sunken, darker and greasy looking. Can you see here?"

He pointed to the black cells on the frame. "The bee larvae inside will be weak from the AFB spores. I'm sorry. I can see from here that looks like American foulbrood."

"Poor bees," Eilidh cried, feeling a sickening sense of dread as she asked the next, inevitable question. "Will we lose the apiary?"

Buzz looked at her levelly. "We will need to destroy this hive, to help stop the spread of infection."

Eilidh nodded numbly. "Will even the honey have to be destroyed?"

"Aye, I'm afraid so."

"Ah," Eilidh said, feeling tearful as her happiness was crushed thinking about all the effort the bees had put into their work this season. All that glorious honey gone to waste…

"How long do we have to wait for the results?" she asked, anxiously.

"I can tell you right away," Buzz replied, and Eilidh felt a glimmer of hope. "There's a field test we can do. An Lfd test, it's similar to a pregnancy test, and it gives us a result right away."

"Thank goodness."

"We take a sample from the cells," Buzz replied as he took a sample and added it to the LFD test."

Eilidh watched the fluid move across the test, watching the control line come up, and saw as the test line came up straight away.

"Oh, Jings," she murmured, her voice breaking.

"Och, I'm so sorry, Lass," Buzz replied. "But at least you can rest assured it is just the one hive."

"Thank you," Eilidh said, feeling her eyes welling with tears.

"I also need to issue a standstill notice. No sales until six weeks time, when I'll come back and check the hives again."

Eilidh nodded numbly.

"Aye, of course. I'll need to destroy the hives right away. I can take over it for you, deal with the hive, and sterilise the whole site for you."

"Thank you," Eilidh said. "I'll let you get on. I'm gonnae head over to the farm and give Angus the news."

"Aye," Buzz replied. "You have your honeymoon to get organised. Dinnae fret about all that. I can help Grace whilst you're away. You dinnae have to worry about anything."

"Thank you."

At Cairnmhor Farm, up on the hillside, Dougie parked the quad bike and walked over to the paddock, where the red deer were quietly grazing.

"Here they are," Dougie said in hushed tones, as he and Jo approached the gate, watching in silence.

"They're braw," Jo murmured back, feeling her heart quicken. "I've never been so close to red deer. They're wonderful."

The cool breeze drifted down the hillside, and for a moment, the deer glanced up, sniffing the air before returning to their grazing.

"They cannae smell us," Dougie replied as they stood together under the shade of the conifer trees. Jo glanced at him. He was taller, broader, with thick biceps, and seemed even more rugged up close. She tried to ignore the definite spark of attraction she felt, as an image of him holding her in his arms sprang into her mind. They'd only just met, and she wasn't over Colin...she glanced away, feeling angry with herself. She shouldn't be letting her ex ruin this lovely moment. This was something she had dreamt of, and it felt lovely to share it with someone who shared the same excitement and wonder that she did.

"These are the hinds. They are currently with their young calves, whom will be weaned from them in August, and then in October, the rut will begin."

"So there's no stag with them now?" Jo asked. "They're like sheep in that case."

"Aye, we tend to separate them or we'd have babies too early in the year."

"Like back home," Jo agreed. "We try and aim for mid April or early May for the lambs. Especially as we breed Vailais Blacknose too."

"Eilidh was saying she'd love to have some of those," Dougie replied.

"They're hardy mountain sheep back in Switzerland but here, it's too muddy and the ground ruins their feet. They need to be indoors a lot."

"Aye, especially in winter, with the storms."

"We've had a bad few the last few years. We had to move the Shetlands down to safer pastures."

"You know a lot about sheep. I bet you'll find livestock a lot easier than you think," Dougie said glancing across at her with a broad grin.

"Sheep, I'm confident about," Jo agreed, with a tilt of her head. "It's the deer and cattle I need some practice with."

"We dinnae have any cattle but my Da knows a cattle farmer. I'll ask him for a few pointers. Cows can be dangerous if rubbed up the wrong way."

"Aye, I heard. That's what makes me feel a wee bit nervous."

"I bet Shetlands can be tough too? I heard that they like to get their own way?"

Jo burst out laughing, nodding. "They're like toddlers in wool coats and with horns! They're very hardy and can be stubborn. My friend who works on a neighbouring farm has a Shetland like that. She's very strong willed and knows her own mind. The sheep, not my friend."

"I like her already!"

"Have you always been in farming?" Jo asked.

"I wanted to be a vet too, actually," Dougie replied. "But I didnae get the grades, and I thought, what's the next best thing? I'd already got a wealth of experience growing up on a farm, following in my Da's footsteps seemed the logical next step. How about you? You didnae want to be a shepherdess?"

"Not really. My parents left that life, left it up to my uncle and aunty. I wanted a bit more variety."

Dougie gave an enthusiastic nod as they fell back to watching the deer for a few moments.

"I have a good question," Jo announced. "If you could work with any animal, what would it be?"

"Och, I've no' thought about that before. A Scottish Wildcat? I'd love to see one up close. You can apparently see them in the wild in the Cairngorms but they're like hen's teeth!"

"There's a wildlife centre back home in Braerannoch where they have wildcats, and they're on the breeding to release programme. I've been a few times and they are beautiful."

"Wow. That sounds wonderful," Dougie replied. "I'll have to take a trip over and see them."

"You should," Jo agreed. His gaze met hers for a few seconds too long, and she suddenly became aware of how close they were standing together, and she felt her heart race a little bit faster. He was really attractive. So friendly and naturally at ease with someone he'd just met. She liked him instantly.

"We should be heading back," she said, feeling her breath quicken in her throat when he didn't move. Maybe he could sense it too…

"Aye, you're right," he said, sounding reluctant, and took a step back. "Follow me back down the path to the quad. It's a wee bit tricky."

They walked back over the dusty path, navigating tree roots and stones, and pine cones, staying in the shade with the heat of the sun, then with Jo sitting on the back, Dougie rode the quad back to the farm.

"Oh, look, Eilidh's back," Jo announced as they reached the lower paddocks and saw Eilidh deep in conversation with Grace.

"Wait, she seems upset, what's going on?"

"Och, hen, that's awful!" Grace was saying as they approached. "I'm so sorry…"

"It'll be alright, Paddington," Angus said, pulling her to him, and holding her protectively.

"Buzz is there right now. I couldnae stay," Eilidh wept.

"What's going on?" Dougie asked, as he and Jo approached.

"I'll go and check on Da and the kids," Grace announced and headed into the farmhouse.

"Eilidh?" Jo asked, and seeing her distraught face, felt her blood run cold.

"I'm so sorry, Jo, we cannae let you have the hives. We've got American foulbrood. It's a virus which affects the larvae in a hive through infectious spores. It's highly contagious amongst the bees and the only way to get rid of it is to…to…"

"The bee inspector has destroy the hive, bees included, and the honey the bees have produced," Angus explained, taking over from Eilidh, who was too distraught to speak. "It has to be burnt, and then buried in the ground to stop any prevalent AFB spores. It can wipe out entire colonies. We're luckily it's just one hive or we could have lost our honey business."

"That's awful!" Jo cried, clapping a hand to her mouth. "Eilidh, I'm so sorry."

"We have a no sales notice to uphold for the next six weeks," Eilidh croaked. "I'm afraid you've had a wasted journey for the bees, Jo. I'll call your aunty and let her know."

"Och, she'll understand," Jo said, stepping forward and patting her shoulder. "I'm here to see Leanna too, so it hasnae been a wasted journey. In fact, I should be getting back to Duck Cottage… unless you need me to stay? Is there anything you can do?"

"No, Jo, you head back. It's verra kind of you to offer," Angus replied with a warm smile.

"I'll give you a lift back if you like?" Dougie suggested.

Jo nodded. "Thank you, that's really kind."

"Thank you," Angus said as they watched Dougie and Jo go.

"Och, Paddington, it'll be alright," Angus soothed her when they'd gone.

"How can we head on honeymoon now? How can I go, knowing our legacy might be destroyed?" Eilidh sobbed, burying her face in his chest. He was grubby from shearing, and smelt of lanolin, grease and dust, and badly in need of a shower, but she didn't care right now. All she wanted and needed was his arms around her.

"Sweetheart, we can get through this. We can deal with everything one step at a time. We can still go on honeymoon. It might be good for us after all this... Shall we head home and I'll make us a brew? Get a takeaway so we dinnae have to cook?"

"Aye, that sounds grand. Extra sugar for me in the tea please. Och, I have to call Rory and let him know everything that's gone on..."

Angus shook his head gently. "We can ask Buzz to do that. And I'll do one better and put a wee dram in your tea for you." He kissed her gently on the forehead. "Dinnae fret about the future. Once we get the all clear after this six week notice, we can look to it then, and things will be alright...I promise."

Chapter Four

"*L*ook, you're gonnae have a wonderful time... like Angus said it will take your mind off everything," Grace assured Eilidh as she and Angus loaded the Land Rover, ready to head off to the harbour to catch the ferry to the mainland. "Are you absolutely sure you've got everything?"

Eilidh nodded. "We've got the passports, credit card, and suitcases."

"Aunty Eilidh! Dinnae worry about the bees," Mhairi piped up. "We shall look after them while you have your honeymoon. Are you gonnae climb the Trifle Tower?"

"Eiffel Tower, no' trifle!" Ollie laughed. "And there are lots of stairs. Aunty Eilidh doesnae have to climb the tower!"

"I think there's a wee lift," Eilidh replied, hugging her and then Ollie before she got in the passenger seat.

"Have a grand time," Grace said pulling her into a maternal hug. "Dinnae fret about the farm, we'll take care of everything whilst you're away."

"Thanks Gracie. I'll bring you back something nice."

"Aye, some exciting news I hope!" Grace crossed her fingers and Angus rolled his eyes. "Hurry now or you'll miss the ferry!"

Eilidh got in the passenger seat and fastened her belt, and Angus beeped the horn, as they waved back, watched by them all, including the dogs, as they drove off down the driveway.

"Feels strange, leaving Mossbrae again," she said half an hour later as she stood on the top deck of the car ferry as they watched Mossbrae getting further and further away. She glanced up at the gathering clouds on the horizon with a frown. "I hope the weather will be a wee bit less stormy looking than here!"

Angus nodded in agreement, taking her hand and giving it a light squeeze. "Aye, but this time, we're doing it together, even if the weather is awful, we're there together."

"We are," she grinned, looking up at him, feeling her heart race as she stared into his dark eyes. He tightened his grip on her hand, to reassure her he wasn't going anywhere, and she blushed at the sight of their wedding rings glinting in the early morning sunlight.

"Are you excited?"

She nodded. "I hardly slept last night, I'm so excited. I'm gonnae be falling asleep by lunchtime! Do you think everyone will cope alright whilst we're away? After the week we've had, it's been like treading on eggshells."

"Dinnae fret about the farm. Grace is more than capable," Angus said. "We're gonnae have a lovely time."

Eilidh turned her attention back to the sea, glad it was only a little choppy today and she breathed in the fresh salty sea air.

"Look!" she called, pointing across at the cliff top in the distance. They both looked over, and saw the speck of the grand red and white lighthouse overlooking the bay below. "Och, it looks so picturesque!"

"It does, aye," Angus replied, putting an arm around her shoulders.

"Excuse me,"

They turned at the sound of one of the stewards. "I'm gonnae have to ask you to head back downstairs to the lower deck. We have to divert the ferry."

"What?" Eilidh gasped. "Why?"

"There's a storm coming. The route to the mainland isnae safe enough to continue."

"Where are we being diverted to?" Angus asked, putting an arm around Eilidh's shoulders.

"Braerannoch, it's the closest harbour on route."

"Well, at least that's no' too far from home," Eilidh conceded. "I'm sure we can get another ferry to the mainland once the storm passes. But what about our flight?"

"We can get another flight," Angus assured her.

They followed the steward downstairs as the ferry changed course, and Eilidh watched the lighthouse getting closer and closer as they sat in the lower deck. At least it would give her a chance to explore Braerannoch, having heard so many lovely things about it from Leanna.

The ferry approached the harbour, and then headed below decks to get into the car and drive up the ramp onto the Main Street.

"What can we do until we get another ferry to the mainland?" Eilidh asked as they set off to explore.

"Shall we find a pub and get some lunch?"

"Leanna was saying there is a pub called The Thistle on the Main Street. Shall we try there?"

They turned right and drove past the honey coloured cottages, until they found The Thistle. They parked up and headed inside, quickly finding a table by the window, when Angus's mobile sprang into life.

"Hello? Grace? Is everything alright? What? Right. Thanks for letting me know," Angus said, his face creasing into a frown as he hung up.

"Is everything alright?" Eilidh asked, feeling a sense of dread. "Is there a problem at home? Is it your Da?"

Angus shook his head. "No, it's no' that. There's an ash cloud heading across Europe and all flights have been cancelled."

"Including ours?"

"I'm gonnae double check," Angus replied. He loaded up his email and let out a long sigh. "Och, it's been cancelled. I'm so sorry, Paddington."

"I cannae believe it!" Eilidh gasped, feeling crushed. "We'll have to head home as soon as we can get a ferry."

"Did you mention ferries?"

They turned to the woman in her late sixties behind the bar. "The ferries have been cancelled until the end of the week because of the storm."

"Cancelled?" Eilidh cried, visibly paling. Would they ever get to go their honeymoon? "So we're stranded here? Where will we stay?"

"Are there any B&Bs here?" Angus called over to the landlady.

"There's a rental cottage up by Elderflower Farm," she replied. "It's about a ten minute drive from here, on the outskirts of the village. Tell them Ursula sent you."

"Thank you. We'll head up and ask them."

"Wait a minute, Elderflower Farm is where Leanna and Jo's aunt and uncle live. Alice and Ray McKinnon. Och, the irony."

"That's wonderful though," Angus said, taking her hand. "We can stay here and look around, see how wonderful Braerannoch is."

Eilidh nodded and she forced a smile. "It suppose we'd best make the most of things…"

After a delicious meal of steak and chips, and having thanked Ursula, they headed to the car and drove along the Main Street, heading out to the outskirts of Braerannoch.

Eilidh glanced out the window and noticed with a feeling of foreboding that the clouds were coming in closer.

They drove up the main road and past the market square. Braerannoch was a lovely little village, with pretty stone cottages, and a large village square, where, she could see now, the flower market was being held today. There were around twenty stalls and as they drove past, Eilidh wound down the window, breathing in the wonderful scent of roses, peonies, that drifted towards them.

"Och, that smells braw!" she exclaimed. "We'll have to have to look later on in the week."

Angus nodded in agreement, and they drove on past a row of shops, a local shop, post office, and veterinary centre.

"That must be where Leanna's sister, Jo works," she added as they drove past.

The shops soon dispersed, and soon they were driving through conifer forests, and then rolling fields of baled hay, so much like Mossbrae, and then, in the distance, she spotted the white farmhouse.

"You have reached your destination," intoned the sat nav as they turned right and up a dusty country lane and through a metal gate.

"This is a lovely set up," Angus said as he admired the fields of sheep as they drove up the drive. "I can see Shetlands in the distance. Och! There are some Vailais Blacknoses!"

He nodded across and Eilidh gasped in delight at the small herd of Valais sheep. They were fluffy and black and white, with grand horns and deep, throaty bleats as the ewes called to each other. They looked adorable. "I wonder if Ray's got any for sale?"

"You want to buy some?" Eilidh asked with a raised eyebrow and he shrugged.

"If only I'd brought the trailer. I did say I was gonnae get you some for a wedding present, as a pet project," he glanced at her, adding with a grin. "I keep saying I'll make a shepherdess out of you yet."

"Well, I have got a sheepdog," Eilidh replied brightly. "I could be a beekeeping shepherdess."

"Aye, that sounds like a grand idea," Angus grinned.

They parked the Land Rover and Eilidh got out, shielding her eyes from the bright sunlight.

"I cannae see anyone. Do you think they're up on the hillside?"

"Try the farmhouse," Angus suggested, waiting as Eilidh made her way across the farmyard.

She rang the bell, and waited, feeling slightly awkward. Inside, there was the distant sound of barking dogs, and Eilidh felt a surge of relief as the door was finally answered.

"Alice?" Eilidh asked as a blonde lady in her early forties answered the door.

"Aye?"

"I'm Eilidh Kincaid. We spoke on the phone last night about the beehives."

"Och, lass, you didnae need to come in person. I'm sorry about to hear about your hives. But what are you doing in Braerannoch? I thought you were off on your honeymoon? Leanna said you were off to Paris?"

"Sadly, it looks like we're taking our honeymoon here instead. Our ferry has been diverted because of a storm coming, and we've just found out our flight to Paris has been cancelled because of an ash cloud."

"Och, that's a terrible shame! Have you anywhere to stay?"

"No, we were hoping you'd be able to help us with that," Angus said. "Ursula at The Thistle was saying you have a holiday cottage that we might be able to stay at?"

"You're in luck, we just had a cancellation," Alice replied and Eilidh felt almost tearful with relief. "The cottage, Seaside Cottage is just across the bay, over there. Can you see the blue cottage across the way?"

They turned, spotting a blue cottage in the distance at the top of the headland, and below were the crashing waves and a pebble beach. It looked wonderful, and Eilidh felt a small surge of excitement about staying there.

"It looks beautiful," Eilidh replied with a small nod.

"Aye, it's small, but good for a couples, and it'll be clean. Let me just get you a hamper with all the essentials we give guests. There are a few goodies in it from our farm."

She went back inside and returned a few moments later with a large wicker hamper.

"Thank you so much, Alice, that's verra kind," Angus replied, taking it from her and putting it in the back of the car.

"I'm really sorry about your honeymoon, and that you're stranded. But Braerannoch is a lovely place to stay. It's very picturesque, even with a storm brewing."

"Thank you, Alice, that's so kind," Eilidh said, gratefully.

"Dinnae fret, hen," she said, handing her the keys and giving Angus directions. "If there are any problems, give us a call and I'll be right over…"

Chapter Five

*S*easide Cottage sat on the headland, a five minute drive around the bay, from Elderflower Farm. It was a white stone cottage, flanked by conifer trees, and rhododendron bushes which were in full bloom. Over in the far distance stood the lighthouse.

"This looks braw," Angus said as they drove up the hill, along the winding path to the cottage, where they parked and got out, admiring the view.

He turned to her now, putting an arm around her shoulders. "I know it's not the honeymoon we hoped to go on, but I think we're gonnae have a good week. Don't you think?"

"Aye," Eilidh agreed, admiring the cottage. The scent of sweet peas growing up the trellis on the wall filled the air and made her smile. Above the door were peach climbing roses which reminded her so much of home it made her feel almost tearful.

"It's a beautiful cottage."

"Aye," Angus grinned at her as he got the case from the car. "It is. Shall we take a look inside?"

Inside the cottage was surprisingly modern, with dark oak floors and decorated with a blue and cream nautical theme. As she reached the living room, which had two leather sofas, a log burner, and was decorated in heritage blue, and had wall to wall windows, and panoramic views of the shingle beach below.

"Look at that view!" Eilidh gasped. "Och! This is lovely!"

Angus sat heavily down on the sofa and patted the seat besides him. Eilidh sat down next to him and he pulled her to him.

"Aye," Angus agreed, joining her for a few moments before he put the suitcase away. "We could take a walk along the beach afore the weather turns."

Eilidh watched the waves in wonder as they crashed against the beach, falling silent for a few moments.

"Are you alright?"

She nodded, but then shook her head, then wiped her eyes as the tears she had tried to hold back, trickling down her cheek. "Och, I'm just thinking about things, about Paris, and the ash cloud. I'm trying not to seem ungrateful at Ray and Alice letting us stay here. But I'm so disappointed that we cannae go to Paris."

"Aye, me too," Angus agreed. "I'm absolutely gutted. But we can always go another time."

"Aye, I know."

"I'm gonnae call Grace and let her know we're staying here. She said the ash cloud is all over the news," he said, dialling the number as he went into the kitchen to get a better signal.

Eilidh turned the TV on to find it was indeed all over the news.

"Och, look at that," she cried, watching the scenes of people at the airport, where it seemed to be absolute chaos. There were scenes of crowds at the airport queues, people standing with luggage, crying babies, and arguing passengers.

It cut to scenes of long queues for buses, people having to wait to be assigned a hotel, and Eilidh felt her heart sink.

"At least we're no' in the airport like those poor folk..." Angus replied, shaking his head.

"Aye. I'm grateful we're no' sleeping in the airport tonight," Eilidh replied, shaking her head. She glanced outside at the waves again, shaking her head. "I cannae believe there's a storm coming. It doesnae feel real..."

"We'll just have to brave it out," Angus replied, switching the tv off to save Eilidh even more upset. "Shall we check out that hamper?"

She nodded, quietly, and Angus went into the galley kitchen, and brought in the hamper, and laid it on the coffee table. He opened it to reveal a bottle of champagne, a box of designer chocolates, heather flavoured biscuits, and a box of loose leafed tea.

"This is lovely!" Eilidh gasped in delight.

"There's even hot chocolate," Angus added with a grin. "I'll go and make us one."

He went into the kitchen and got two mugs out of the cupboard. "Och, Alice is wonderful. There's bread, milk and butter in here too."

"That's grand," Eilidh replied as Angus brought the hot chocolates into the living room.

He sat down on the sofa, handing her the hot chocolate.

Eilidh took a grateful sip, as Angus put an arm around her shoulders.

"Here's to our honeymoon," he said, clinking his mug against hers. "I know it's no' the honeymoon we hoped for, but here's to a nice time."

Eilidh could not help but smile. "Aye. Here's to our honeymoon."

Angus put his cup down and leant forward, resting one elbow on the sofa, his gaze meeting hers. He was wearing a dark emerald-green polo shirt, and as her gaze took in his muscular forearms, Eilidh felt her heart race at the sight of him.

"Beats paying for a hotel mini bar," she joked, to break the tension.

"Aye, it does," Angus gave a soft chuckle.

"You're staring…" Eilidh said, blushing.

"Aye, I know, I like the view," he grinned, and leant forwards, kissing her on the mouth. It was a dry kiss, but she could feel the passion bubbling beneath the surface, and it was all she could do not to tug his shirt off right then and there.

Angus put an arm around her waist, pulling her to him, and gently took the vase, putting it on the counter as he pulled her into a deeper kiss. He tasted of hot chocolate, toothpaste and mouthwash, and she breathed in the scent of his after-shave, and felt her head spin with happiness.

"Since we're on honeymoon, why don't we get make the most of it? Which way is the bedroom?"

Angus's face broke into a grin, and he stood up, taking her hand.

"Let's do this properly," he scooped her up into his arms, making her squeal as he carried her along the narrow hallway towards the bedroom, ready to celebrate their honeymoon properly…

Chapter Six

 *T*he early morning sunlight streamed in through the bay windows as Eilidh sat in the window seat, watching the waves crashing on the beach down below.

"Braw morning isn't it?" Angus said as he walked in with two teas. "You're up early."

"Aye, I couldnae sleep," she replied, gesturing to the book she was holding. Not too much of a reader given she hardly ever had time, Eilidh was making an effort to get back into reading, starting with the classics, and for the occasion, how fitting was her second hand copy of Thomas Hardy's Far From the Madding Crowd. She had just started, but distracted by the waves below, put the book down, and glanced out of the window.

"I think the sea's getting a little more fierce…"

"Aye, do you fancy a walk on the beach afore we get swept away?"

"That'd be lovely," Eilidh replied. "We could go for a drive, and explore the village. I wonder if they do the flower market every day? I'd like to get Alice some flowers to say thank you for letting us stay."

"We could always ask her. Fancy some breakfast? I think Alice has also left us some eggs."

"Sounds braw," Eilidh grinned.

"You look beautiful. Lack of sleep suits you," Angus said with a wink.

"Thank you. You too," Eilidh said, meeting his gaze and blushed, thinking back to their night last night.

After scrambled eggs on toast, and more tea, Eilidh and Angus headed out down the coastal path down to the beach.

"It's like where we had our first kiss," she sighed with happiness, pausing as she admired the view, the crashing waves against the shingle beach, reminding her so much of the scenes she had just been reading.

"Aye?" Angus asked, taking her in his arms and pulling her into a deep, passionate kiss. For a moment, for Eilidh, time stood still, as they held each other, lost in nostalgia, until a sudden gust of wind whipped her hair around her face, and she pulled away, laughing.

"I should have worn a hat! I'm all windswept!"

"Och, you look beautiful no matter what."

There was a frenzied barking as a border collie came racing across the beach chasing a ball, barking excitedly.

Angus beckoned the dog over who dropped the ball.

"I see he's made some more friends!"

They turned to see a tall, redheaded man walking towards them. He was wearing a checked shirt and shorts, and whistled to the dog who turned and raced back towards him.

"He's lovely," Eilidh called.

"Aye, he's a grand dog."

"Sheepdog?"

The man nodded. "He is. Are you two the couple who called at the farm yesterday?"

"Aye, we are," Angus agreed. "I'm Angus, and this is my wife, Eilidh."

"I'm Ray. You met my wife Alice. Sorry to hear about your honeymoon. Are you finding the cottage comfortable?"

"Aye, very much, thank you," Eilidh nodded, trying not to blush as an image of last night leapt into her mind.

"Grand," Ray replied with a nod. "Braerannoch is a grand place to have a holiday, or indeed a honeymoon. There's a lot to explore."

"Aye, it's a lovely place. We were thinking of exploring afore the storm hits. Is the flower market on every day?" Eilidh asked.

"Aye, it is, although today will be the last day as the storm is gonnae hit tomorrow. I've to get the Shetlands in from the hills."

"They're a hardy breed," Angus agreed.

"Aye, need to be living here," Ray replied with a nod. "How about yourselves? I hear you run a farm back home in Mossbrae?"

Angus nodded. "We run Scottish Blackface and red deer."

"Aye? We saw you have an online shop. That's impressive." Ray replied.

"Aye, we sell lamb, venison, and honey. We also sell hampers."

"We were having a look on the website," Ray said, enthusiastically. "Alice has already been online and wants to buy some honey."

"Ah, that would be lovely. We do ship as well."

"Aye, I'll bear that in mind," Ray replied. "We also breed Swiss Vailais Blacknose sheep. They're really popular as pets."

"Aye, we were thinking of getting some Vailas sheep too,"

Angus said, glancing at Eilidh. "I'm trying to get this one into shepherding, and she's already got a pup, so we just need some sheep. I promised her some as a wedding present."

"Aye, well you're more than welcome to come over and take a look around the farm, and if you want any ewes, I can bring them to you once the ferries start running again."

"Och, that's grand of you, Ray, thanks so much."

Ray nodded and then, glanced up at the darkening sky, his face creasing into a frown. "Och, looks like this storm is headed in, aye?"

Eilidh looked up, nodding in agreement. "We ought to go on our tour afore the storm hits."

Ray nodded. "If you need anything, let us know. Oh, and Alice wondered if you'd like to come over for dinner tonight? To welcome you to Braerannoch."

"That would be lovely, thank you."

"No worries. Come over around six pm," Ray replied.

"Aye, thank you. See you there."

"See you tonight," Ray smiled, and whistled to Brock, and made his way back up the beach, towards Elderflower Farm.

Braerannoch was a tiny village, more of a hamlet, really, as Eilidh and Angus drove over the bridge and back into the village. It was a pretty, picturesque little place, chocolate boxy, Eilidh thought, as they drove past a row of honey coloured houses, and a post office on their left. On the right was a road leading to the market square, and a small super-market, flanked on both sides by more houses. The Main Street, Eilidh thought, seemed to be the only road leading in and out of Braerannoch. Nevertheless, she was impressed.

"Look, they're setting up," Eilidh exclaimed, pointing over to the market square, to where the vendors were laying out buckets of flowers in wooden chalet style stalls. They'd look wonderful at Christmas, she thought, as Angus turned right and parked in the car park.

"Aye, reminds me of home," Angus said wistfully, and Eilidh turned to him with a smile.

"Homesick already?"

"Not just yet," Angus grinned as they got out, and walked towards the market.

As they did, Eilidh was enveloped with a mist of scents, roses, peonies, dahlias, and it made her head spin with happiness. Looking around, she glanced at the stalls, taking in the fresh flowers and found she couldn't keep the smile off her face.

"Wonderful, aye?" Angus smiled.

"It's magnificent," she breathed, feeling like she was walking through a dream.

She walked over to a stall filled with roses, and admired them all. They were clearly freshly cut, in full bloom and heady with sweet, honey-scented fragrance. It was like being at home in the honey shed when she did the extractions.

"What do you think to these ones?" She asked, glancing at Angus.

"Aye, they're braw," Angus replied.

"We specialise in homegrown flowers here in Braerannoch, sourcing flowers grown in the Highlands," piped in the stall owner, a short, grey haired woman with crooked teeth and bright blue eyes, and Eilidh glanced up to see it was Ursula.

"Hello again!" She cried. "Did you find Elderflower Farm alright?"

"Aye, we did," Eilidh replied. "Alice is kindly letting us to stay at Seaside Cottage."

"Och, that's wonderful," Ursula said.

"I'm looking for some roses to get her as a thank you."

"Alice loves yellow roses," Ursula replied. "They're her favourite."

"Thank you. In that case I'll get these please."

"Aye, they're my favourite too," Ursula smiled. "So how are you settling in?"

"It's wonderful," Eilidh replied. "We're taking the opportunity to explore the village afore the storm hits."

"Well, we have theme nights at the Thistle if you're looking for something to do. There's one on tomorrow night, in fact. You're most welcome to drop in."

"Thank you, that's really kind," Eilidh replied, turning to Angus, who nodded enthusiastically. "We'll see you there."

Eilidh paid for the flowers and they headed back to the car just as it was starting to drizzle and there was a faint rumble of thunder in the distance.

"Och," Angus tutted, glancing up. "Looks like the storm's on it's way here."

"Aye, it does," Eilidh agreed as they got into the car and Angus started the engine, and headed off to Elderflower Farm.

"Thank you so much, they're braw!" Alice gasped as Eilidh handed her the flowers. "I love yellow roses. I'll just put them in some water."

She hurried into the kitchen and put them in water, then returned, wiping her damp hands on her blue and white striped apron.

"Come on through. Would you like a drink? I have some home made elderflower wine if you'd like some?"

Angus and Eilidh followed Alice into the farmhouse.

Inside, the farmhouse was surprisingly modern, with hardwood floors and high ceilings, and a grand Aga in the middle of the kitchen, with a vast bouquet of roses in the centre, which Eilidh could see from the hallway.

"That sounds braw, thank you," Eilidh replied, as Alice ushered them through to the living room where Ray was sitting in a faded armchair, with Brock snoring happily at his feet.

"Ah, you made it," Ray said with a broad smile. "Lovely to see you again."

"And you," Angus said, as they sat on the sofa, feeling instantly relaxed and welcome.

"Here's the wine," Alice called as she handed them each a glass of clear, fizzy liquid, which smelt delicious.

Eilidh took a tentative sip. It was sweet, and she felt the bubbles burst on her tongue. It was wonderful.

"Och, that's lovely," she gasped. "I must get the recipe from you."

"Of course," Alice grinned. "So you've had chance to look around Braerannoch. What do you think?"

"It's a lovely village," Eilidh enthused.

"Have you been to the wildlife centre? It's on the outskirts and you can have a look around. They've got Wildcats."

"Really?" Eilidh enthused, exchanging an excited glance at Angus.

"We can go and take a look around. I've never seen a Wildcat."

"Aye, and they're working to release them back into the wild," Alice added.

"That's fantastic," Eilidh enthused.

"In the meantime, Angus, you said you were interested in seeing the sheep," Ray announced, getting out of the armchair. "Fancy a wee look around the shed whilst we're waiting for dinner?"

"Aye, that would be lovely," Angus replied and they all followed him out.

"Won't we be making you wait for dinner?" Eilidh asked Alice anxiously but she shook her head jovially.

"Och, no. We've chicken and leek pie for dinner. It'll keep hot in the Aga."

"In that case, let's go."

"Did you have a good morning exploring the village?" Ray asked as they walked across the farm yard towards the barn at the far side.

Angus nodded. "Aye, it's lovely village."

"It's like a home from home," Eilidh added. "We got talking to Ursula earlier at the flower market, and we're going to check out the theme night at the Thistle."

"Och, they're a lot of fun, those theme nights!" Alice exclaimed. "We go to every one!"

"The Shetlands are up on the hillside just now," Ray explained, as he pushed open the barn door. "But we have the Valais in here. There are a few older lambs, and the ewes. They are a wee bit sensitive to the cold weather, despite being from Sweden."

"They are beautiful," Eilidh breathed, taking in the ewes now, who, by all accounts looked like toys, with their thick curly fleeces and even curlier horns. They were mostly white, with black knee patches and muzzles, and the lambs looked exactly like they'd been knitted from the softest alpaca or kid silk wool.

"Aye, this is a grand set up!" Angus exclaimed.

"Aye, we manage well, but it's good to have two barns, especially with the weather," Ray replied.

The barn, was a wide open space, with a vaulted ceiling, and plenty of light despite it being a cloudy afternoon.

"The Valais Blacknose is a Swiss breed. They are hardy but don't do mud and wet too well, their feet are quite delicate," Ray explained.

"Do they need a lot of shearing?" Angus asked, as he admired them. "They look braw! I love the twisted horns."

"Aye, they are particularly impressive. Both the ewes and rams have horns, but the rams's horns are truly impressive. This is our ram, Herb. He's responsible for all the lambs and he's a kind, gentle giant."

He pointed to the ram now, a huge animal with a thick, long, heavy fleece and massive curled horns giving him an almost wild sheep appearance, making him look like a cuddly toy.

"I can see now why they get called the cutest sheep in the world," Eilidh said.

"Aye, wait until you see the lambs over here," Ray announced, and lead them over to the lambing pen which was full of cute fluffy lambs. "They're a few months old now, but they're still wee and fluffy."

"Och, they're adorable!" She cooed.

"They are often sold as pets," Ray continued. "There's been a surge for them as pets in recent years. But they aren't cheap sheep. They cost quite a lot for a pure Swiss line ewe and rams are even more expensive."

"Aye, is that so? How expensive are they?"

"At least fifteen hundred pounds for a ewe, even more for a ram. They're a rare breed you see. We've only had them for the last seven years since they had been brought into the UK."

"That's fascinating!" Eilidh enthused.

"Aye, there's only around 19,000 of them in the world," Ray continued.

"Och, it makes me wish we'd brought the trailer so we could get some," Angus said glancing at Eilidh. "What do you think? I did say I was gonnae get you some as a wedding present."

"Maybe once the ash cloud has gone and all this has passed, we could get a couple," she agreed.

"We could bring them to you once the storm has passed," Ray replied. They left the shed, just as the rain arrived, falling so hard it bounced off the ground.

"Och! I think that's our cue to get indoors. Let's head in, dinner will almost be ready," Alice announced and they all headed back to the farmhouse.

After a delicious dinner of a wonderful chicken and leek pie with crumbly, buttery, flakey pastry, steamed broccoli, green beans and mashed potatoes.

"That was braw," Eilidh gasped. "I cannae eat another bite!"

"Och, I hope you've room enough for a raspberry carnation!"

"Of course," Angus replied, with a grin.

"Grand," Alice beamed and headed back into the kitchen, coming back in with the cranachan.

It was sweet, fruity and delicious, a mix of fresh cream, raspberries and raspberry sauce, a summer classic.

Eilidh nodded. "Please can I have the recipe for that too?"

"Aye, of course," Alice chuckled.

"Thank you so much for dinner," Eilidh replied. "We really should be heading back to the cottage."

"Aye," Alice replied. "It's been a pleasure having you."

She glanced out of the window and blew air out of the side of her mouth. "I see the rain has arrived, and it appears the wind has got up."

Angus nodded, and put an arm around Eilidh's shoulders, as they bid goodbye.

"We'll maybe see you in the Thistle tomorrow. It's karaoke night!" Alice added with a grin.

"Karaoke?" Eilidh exchanged a glance with Angus. "Ursula didnae mention that!"

"Och, we love our karaoke here in Braerannoch," Alice replied. "Some of the villagers take it quite seriously! Make sure you practice your singing voice! It's gonnae be a great craic!"

Chapter Seven

The following morning, the waves were increasingly choppy as Eilidh and Angus set out exploring the rest of Braerannoch before the storm hit.

"I hope the karaoke isnae a washout tonight," Eilidh joked as they drove along the country lanes.

"It willnae be," Angus assured her. "I've been practicing."

"Aye, I heard you in the shower this morning!"

Angus turned to her with a raised eyebrow. "Were you impressed?"

Eilidh met his gaze, and nodded. "You're gonnae do me proud tonight. Team Kincaid all the way!"

Angus took her hand and kissed it quickly. "Which way is this wildlife centre?"

"It should be down this next turning on the left," Eilidh replied.

They took the next left turning and drove up a gravelled drive into the car park. Ahead of them was an unassuming red brick building, which read BRAERANNOCH WILDLIFE

CENTRE. Once a farmhouse, it had been converted and was now a visitor centre with an adjoining cafe.

"I cannae wait to see the wildcats," Eilidh said with childish excitement as they walked in hand in hand through the green double doors of the entrance. Inside, it opened up to wide open space, painted elm green and chestnut brown to mirror the conifer forests surrounding the centre. In the middle of the room there was a visitor desk, and to the right, was a modest gift shop selling books and souvenirs.

Over to the left in a room which looked like a long, rectangular conservatory with floor to ceiling windows, was a tea room, and even from here they could see the gorgeous views. The tea room was clean and modern, with green plastic chairs, and square matching tables decorated with a posy of fresh flowers and a menu. Eilidh could smell freshly made scones and heard the tea and coffee machine hiss and whirr, and her stomach growled longingly.

"Morning," the girl at reception greeted them warmly. "Are you wanting to take a look around?"

"If that's alright?" Eilidh asked tentatively.

"Aye, of course, head on through," said the girl, handing them a map and a guidebook.

They headed outside to the main centre, and saw to their delight that there were dozens of enclosures looping around in a circle, and branching off to other parts of the centre. Eilidh glanced around, marvelling at how beautiful it was here. It was a fresh, breezy day, but quiet and tranquil was the same time.

"They're just like the ones we have a home," she exclaimed as they waited by the red deer enclosure on their left. The herd, made up of six hinds and one stag, was quiet and calm, enjoying their breakfast.

"Magnificent," Angus agreed, and glanced at Eilidh.

Eilidh looked at the guide book. "Apparently, these deer are rescues, they were orphaned and hand reared.

"Well they appear to have a good home here," Angus replied, as they moved on, heading up the gravel path towards two large enclosures which flanked the path.

"It says here," Eilidh continued, "the centre opened almost ten years ago, and they used to be an entirely indoor centre, with a tiny tearoom, and a few enclosures. They didnae have any big animals like the ones they have today. Seven years ago, they expanded, and were able to move all our animals outdoors, add on the cafe to the tearoom, and turn Braerannoch Wildlife centre into the centre that's here today."

She gestured to the enclosures. "Here's the Highland Takin, they are a species of antelope. There should be a pair in here."

"Wonderful," Angus sighed, as they took in the pair, with their thick woolly coats and curling horns.

"Up here, there's the aviaries," Eilidh went on, and they walked further up the hill to see hand reared Golden Eagles, Eagle Owls and Red Kites.

Then, they walked back down the other side of the hill, towards a wooded area.

"Apparently, there are red squirrels and wildcats this way," Eilidh said excitedly. "did you know Scottish Wildcats are also known as the Highland Tiger?"

She lead the way through the wooded area, where there were three large enclosures. On the right stood a fenced off area, flanked by conifer trees. Inside were red squirrels, who were wild but were fed by the staff at the wildlife centre. They paused outside the enclosure, waiting with bated breath. Then, a few squirrels came to the feeder, a tray fixed to the trees, and they watched in delight, at the tiny red squirrels who looked like Beatrix Potter illustrations, as they fed, groomed each other, and went about their business as though they weren't even there.

"The wildcats are over here," Eilidh announced with childish enthusiasm, as they walked to the top enclosure. "This centre is also working with Wildcat Conservation and Breeding Programme, and takes in rescued wildcats, with the intention of breeding and rereleasing them back into the wild."

"That's amazing," Angus enthused as they reached the wildcat enclosures. Both enclosures were in a wooded area, with a lot of foliage to shelter the cats and keep them as secretive as they hoped to be. There were also wire runs above their heads as they looked up, with shelters for the cats, so that they could walk up high if they wanted to between their enclosures. Eilidh felt her heart race with excitement, admiring the surroundings and thinking if she were a Wildcat, she would love to live here.

"This is Pixie, and her kittens, Bruce and Logan," Angus said, reading the information board near the enclosure.

"Och, they're braw!" Eilidh gasped, as she glanced up and saw the mother cat and kittens directly above her head. The cat regarded her silently, her vivid green eyes meeting hers, as the cat regarded Eilidh coolly. Eilidh felt her heart race as she gazed back, knowing just how rare these cats were and how lucky she was to see one up close in the flesh. The kittens were tiny, and they hissed a little, bright eyes fixed on her.

"Aye," Angus whispered. "Shame they are so rare now. According to this, it's chiefly due to loss of habitat and hybridisation. These cats here are almost ninety percent pure-bred wildcat, and they're hoping to increase that percentage through their kittens, so that they may be able to survive in the wild."

"I've never seen one so close before," Eilidh gasped. "They're amazing. I feel so privileged."

"Aye," Angus breathed, putting an arm around her and smiling at her as they relished the moment together. "So do I."

He turned to her. "So what do you think about expanding the farm a bit more? The diversity might bring in some more money."

"Aye, that's a grand idea, but I was thinking of expanding…in a different direction," Eilidh replied, turning to him now, a small smile on her face.

"Aye?" Angus asked hopefully. "Are you…"

Eilidh shook her head. "No, not yet. But I was thinking, now we're on honeymoon… we could start thinking about it properly? What do you think?"

"I think," Angus replied, wrapping his arms around her. "That's a braw idea. How about we start planning that tonight, after the karaoke?"

"I like that idea very much," Eilidh grinned and reached up as he put his arms around her, pulling her into a deep, passionate kiss.

The moment was so wonderful they didn't hear the faint distant rumble of thunder.

~

By the time Eilidh and Angus reached The Thistle that evening, it had already begun to rain, and there was an ominous rumble of thunder in the distance.

Eilidh glanced up, seeing the darkening clouds as they hurried along the Main Street. "I hope it gives us chance to get back to the cottage later."

Angus put a protective arm around her. "We'll be back in time. Are you nervous about the singing?"

"Very!"

"We'll be grand!"

They walked into the pub and were immediately enveloped by noise and a throng of people. Inside, the interior was cosy and chic, reminding Eilidh with a pang of homesickness of The Dog and Duck. All that was missing was The Trinity. Over in the far corner was the dance floor, where there was a karaoke machine had been set up. Everywhere else was filled to the brim with people, and it was already two deep at the bar.

They found a booth in a tiny corner of the pub by the log fire.

"This is cosy," Angus grinned, and Eilidh nodded in agreement. Nestled in the booth, surrounded by the crowds, chatter and laughter, made her feel right at home, and she took a moment to admire the decor: leather furniture, cream and coffee coloured walls, hung with quirky paintings of dogs and rabbits, with tartan cushions, and at the centre, a huge log fire. It almost looked like someone's living room instead of a pub.

"I was just thinking the same."

Angus reached for her hand and gave it a squeeze. "Shall we get some dinner afore the karaoke starts?"

"Aye, I'm starving!"

She picked up a menu, scanning it excitedly. "The seafood risotto looks fantastic. Oh, they've got raspberry cranachan!"

"We'll have that then, if you like," Angus replied.

"So, what are we gonnae sing for the karaoke?"

"I've got a song in mind," Angus replied with a soft smile, and then he slid out of the booth. "I'll go and order."

By the time their food arrived, and they were settled with two glasses of white grape Shloer, the karaoke was setting up. She could see there was already a crowd forming, and knew it was going to be busy evening.

"This risotto is delicious!" Eilidh exclaimed as she tucked in. It was deeply flavoured, with prawns, crab and smoked salmon, chives and lemon, creamy, but with that bite which Eilidh loved.

"Right, everyone, the karaoke is about to begin!" Ursula announced into the microphone as the pub paused to listen. "Now, we have a playlist, and you can either choose your own song, as a single singer, or as a duet. So let's begin. Let's give a big round of applause for our first singer!"

The pub erupted into applause as the first singer stepped forward and launched into an enthusiastic performance of Whitney Houston's Dance with Somebody.

Eilidh and Angus, wrapped up in the fun, paused, and clapped along, loving being in the heart of the community.

"Shall we?" Eilidh asked, once they had finished their meal and had listened through a quirky duet of I Got You, a feisty version of I Would Do Anything for Love and a dazzling cover of Don't Stop Me Now.

"Aye, go on then," Angus replied, finishing his drink, and they walked over to the dance floor as the song came to an end and there was rapturous applause.

"Who do we have next?" Ursula asked, as Eilidh and Angus reached the microphone.

"Eilidh and Angus."

"Have you ever sung karaoke before?"

"No!" Eilidh giggled. "But we've been practicing our singing."

"What are you going to sing?" Ursula asked. "Are you gonnae sing a song each, or a duet?"

"We're gonnae sing one each," Angus replied.

"And what do you want to sing?"

"Och, I'm gonnae have to look through the playlist," Eilidh said and Ursula handed her it. "Angus?"

"The Most Beautiful Girl in the World," Angus replied, looking at her, and Eilidh felt her eyes welling with happy tears.

"Right, that's grand!" Ursula announced. "Angus will be singing The Most Beautiful Girl in the World. Take it away, Angus!"

There was a loud round of applause, as the opening notes of the song began, and the lyrics came up on the screen.

"Could you be the most beautiful girl in the world?" Angus began, his voice a soft Baritone compared with Prince's higher voice, as he met Eilidh's gaze, and held it as he sang. "It's plain to see, you're the reason that God made a girl…"

Eilidh glanced around at the audience, feeling her heart race with happiness and excitement. Here she was, enveloped in this welcoming, fun community, surrounded by people who loved Angus singing as much as she did, and she felt her eyes filling with happy tears.

"Och, they made it!" Alice murmured to Ray as they entered the pub and saw Angus singing. "What a lovely song to sing! Och, look at wee Eilidh's face. She looks so happy!"

"Aye, he's a good singer," Ray agreed as he ordered went to the bar and ordered the drinks. "He's got a great baritone."

"And if the stars ever fell from the sky, I know that Mars, could not be too far behind," Angus continued. "Cause this kind of view ain't got no reason to ever be shy..."

"The real question will be if he can hit that high note," Alice continued. "Now if he can do that, I'll be more than impressed!"

A few lines later, and they had their answer, as the final chorus came round and Angus hit the high note with only slight difficulty, but judging by Eilidh's face, he didn't care one bit.

"Och, you could strike a match between those two!" Alice chuckled, clucking like a hen. "It's plain to see the love between them!"

Ray nodded, sipping his beer. "We were like that once, hen," he added, putting an arm around her waist.

"Och, what do you mean?" Alice chided. "We still are!"

They glanced over at the dance floor now as Angus took Eilidh in his arms and kissed her to rapturous applause.

"That was amazing!" Eilidh whispered in his ear, blushing, as he had his arm around her. "I've changed my mind. I dinnae want to sing now."Are you sure?" Angus asked.

She nodded. "I just want to celebrate you. You were fantastic!"

"Thanks," Angus said, with a shy smile.

"I love you."

"I love you too," he replied, looking deeply into her eyes, as though it was only her and him in the pub. "I always have, and I always will."

Chapter Eight

"The rain is coming down now!" Angus murmured as they drove back to Seaside Cottage. The rain was hammering against the windscreen now, and even with the windscreen wipers sweeping across the screen, the screen was blurred with rain. Eilidh felt a jolt of fear, hoping they would get back soon, as Angus was forced to slow down. She jumped as there was an ominous rumble of thunder and lightening flashed across the sky.

They reached the road along the cliff top leading down to the cottage.

"Och, look at the waves!" Eilidh cried, glancing down. The waves were crashing wildly against the beach, and she looked away quickly as it made her feel seasick. "I hope that Alice and Ray are alright."

She glanced across at Elderflower Farm. "Should we check on them afore we turn in?"

"Och, it's a wee bit late now. They'll probably be in bed. They left ages afore we did," Angus replied, glancing at the clock.

It was almost midnight.

Angus parked, and they hurried inside.

"Shall I put the fire on, or shall we just call it a night? It's a wee bit chilly in here," he asked as Eilidh tugged off her coat and kicked off her shoes.

"Let's go straight to bed!"

"Oh, really?" He caught up with her and pulled her into a deep kiss and she felt her heart burst with happiness as she wrapped her arms around him, pulling him closer into the kiss, and with a giggle, started to take off her pink sweater. "So we're no' sleeping yet then?"

"I'm not tired."

"Me neither," Angus said, grinning at her wolfishly, and started to tug off his own T-shirt when a loud hammering at the door made them both pause.

"Angus? Eilidh? Are you there? Are you home?" A frantic voice called, and they both tugged their clothes back on before Angus pulled the door open.

"Och, I'm so sorry," Alice, her face soaked with rain and looking desperate and tearful, was standing on the steps. "I need your help. I cannae reach anyone else, the storm is coming down too strong."

"What's happened?" Eilidh cried, tugging her own clothes back on, seeing the despair on her face.

"It's the Shetlands. Ray had gone out to bring them in. They spooked and now they're lost. Ray sent Brock out to find them, but now they're trapped out on the hillside, and he cannae find them to get them in. He's gone out on the quad bike. Would you be able to help?"

"Of course," Angus replied without a moment's hesitation.

"I'll come with you," Eilidh added. "I can drive a quad bike too, if you need me to."

"Thank you so much!" Alice cried, sounding tearful with

relief as they climbed into their car and followed Alice's Land Rover back to Elderflower Farm, which was a slow journey as they crept back along the coastal path in the gale force winds.

As they reached the brow of the hill, Angus scanned the field, trying to see Ray's distinctive red raincoat with the headlights, or the headlights of the quad bike.

"Ray!" He called out of the window, trying in vain to hear his voice above the driving rain and howling wind, but his efforts were futile. "Jings! This storm isnae helping us!"

There was a crash of thunder, and a flash of lightening streaked across the sky.

"Might be easier to look for Brock in this weather," he murmured. "If we cannae find Ray first."

"There he is!" Eilidh cried, pointing across at the far end of the field, where Ray was driving towards them on the back of his quad bike.

"Och, thank God he's alright!" Alice cried.

Ray drove towards them, pulling to a halt.

"The sheep are scattered!" Ray shouted above the driving rain. "I've sent Brock after them, but they're both lost."

"Dinnae fret," Angus called back. "Me and Eilidh are here to help. We'll try and find Brock."

There was a faint sound of barking, and they all glanced to the right where there was the blurry shape of Brock, as another rumble of thunder made everyone jump. As a flash of lightening streaked across the sky, there was the sound of frantic bleating, and the thundering of hooves.

"That direction!" Alice cried and they turned to see the flock of sheep hurrying down the hillside, followed by Brock. "They're heading for the cliff!"

Angus swore under his breath as he and Ray drove after them. Ray drove in an arc, trying to get the other side of the herd to divert them.

The herd picked up pace, and Angus pressed his foot on the accelerator, trying to get them away from the cliff edge.

"Brock!" Ray called, backing up the command with a piercing whistle, trying to get the dog to hear him.

"We should have brought the dogs!" Angus called to Eilidh, as they reached to the front of the herd, which, luckily, stuck together, as Brock raced ahead, moving round the herd to keep them together.

The driving rain was almost blinding now, turning the field into a quagmire with mud. The cliff edge was getting even closer as Brock, covered in mud, tried to turn the panicked flock.

Ray whistled again, as he reached the cliff edge. Down below, the waves were crashing against the beach. Angus slowed, and drove the Land Rover at a creeping pace around the herd, moving them away from the cliff edge, as thunder crashed over their heads.

Eilidh and Alice sat with bated breath as they drove perilously close to the cliff edge, and managed, slowly, slowly, to move the herd away from the cliff edge and back towards the middle of the film.

Eilidh breathed a sigh of relief, as Ray and Angus, on either side of the herd, drove them back across the field towards the gate at the other side. Ray sped up, and drove the herd towards the gate, hopping off to open the gate as Angus pushed them on.

· · ·

Soon, they were all heading down the hillside, back towards the farm, and before long, the flock were back to the safety of the barn.

"Och, well, that was an eventful evening!" Eilidh announced, a short while later, as she and Angus were snuggled up in bed, drinking hot chocolate.

"Aye, you can say that again!" Angus replied. "Although, we should be saying morning. It's almost three am."

"We ought to get some sleep," Eilidh replied, laying back and stifling a yawn.

"Aye, you're right...But I had another idea," Angus agreed, putting his hot chocolate to one side and turning to her.

Eilidh crooked an eyebrow. "Is that so?"

Angus leant down and kissed her slowly. He tasted of hot chocolate as Eilidh wrapped her arms around his neck and pulled him closer.

"I love you," she said as he peeled off his T-shirt and took her in his arms.

"I love you too," he replied between kisses.

"Wait, I've got a surprise for you."

"Can it wait?" Angus asked.

"No. Look up."

Angus looked up at the ceiling to see a sprig of mistletoe hanging from the bedframe.

"It's for luck."

"Luck?" Angus asked with a light frown.

"Aye," Eilidh replied. "You're so generous and sweet and

lovely. I wanted to give us both some luck, after the conversations we've been having about trying for a baby."

"Och, Paddington," Angus said gently, tucking a stray hair behind her ear. "I dinnae need luck with you. I'm lucky to have you. That's all the luck we need. Now, shall we see if it works?"

Then, he pulled her to him again, kissing her until she felt dizzy with desire, as the storm quietened until only the pattering sound of rain could be heard outside, alongside the crashing of the waves against the beach below.

Chapter Nine

$\mathcal{M}$ ossbrae

At Cairnmhor Farm, the scent of roast beef filled with kitchen as Grace took the joint out of the oven.

"Ah, that's braw," she grinned as she set it to rest on the side. "Who can resist that? It's gorgeous! Ollie, would you go and help Mhairi set the table?"

Ollie ran off to the set the table as Grace checked the roast potatoes, which looked golden and crispy and delicious.

As it was another hot afternoon, they were eating in the garden, to take in the view of the rolling fields in the distance. The wrought iron table sat under the shade of an oak tree, and reminded Grace happily of when Eilidh had first returned to Mossbrae for Robyn's wedding.

"Do you think this is gonnae work?" Robyn asked as she made the gravy. "I know she and Dougie seemed to get on yesterday when they went to see the deer, but can we hope it'll develop into something more? She's only just single. Maybe we need some honey mead."

"Whisht!" Grace hissed. "No thanks, that mead is far too

potent. Eilidh can testify to that! Remember when you gave her some on her birthday and she fell and broke her toes?"

"Och it was two sips!" Robyn chuckled. "But it gave her and Angus chance to get some quality time together."

"Dinnae fret about Jo and Dougie," Grace said. "It's well known that friendship is the best foundation for a successful relationship, so we'll start that off this afternoon. If they sit together, they will get a chance to get to know each other better. There's gorgeous weather, delicious food and good company, so there's no pressure. It'll be good for Jo to have more friends here besides Leanna. It's a chance to make her feel welcome, and make friends, and the same for Dougie. It gives him needs another reason to stay."

"Aye, I couldnae think of a better one," Robyn agreed as the doorbell rang.

"Och, that'll be Jo and Leanna."

Robyn went to answer.

"Hello! Come through, we're eating in the garden."

They followed her through the kitchen.

"Something smells delicious!" Leanna called.

"Thank you," Grace replied. "Your dress is bonny!"

"Thank you," Leanna beamed, smoothing her yellow and green print dress.

"Do you want a drink?" Grace asked, as she reached in the cupboard for glasses.

"We made some lemonade!" Mhairi called from the garden. "Grandda helped." She beamed across at Joe, who was sitting in a deck chair on the patio, enjoying a brew.

"Aye," he called back. "And you did a grand job!"

"Lemonade would be lovely, thank you," Leanna replied, and Mhairi beamed, red curly hair bouncing around her shoulders.

"Have a seat!" Grace called. "Dinner will be out in a few minutes."

Mhairi dashed forward and straightened the cutlery. "Leanna, you're sitting near Ma,"

"Where am I sitting?" Jo asked, walking over, as she pulled her long dark hair into a neat bun. She was wearing jeans and a light pink top, a delicate gold necklace sat at the base of her throat.

"Would you like to sit with me?"

"Aye, that'd be lovely, thank you," Jo replied.

"I like your necklace," Mhairi beamed.

"Thank you."

"Would you like to come and meet our ducks?" Mhairi asked eagerly. "We can feed them if you like?"

"After dinner," Grace chided gently. "We're about to eat."

"Aye, after dinner sounds grand," Jo replied, as she took a seat, admiring the garden.

The doorbell rang again and there was a gaggle of voices.

"Hello!" Maudie's voice echoed in the hallway. "Och, roast beef. I havnae had roast beef for ages!"

"I'll be sure to give you the best potatoes," Grace assured her in a conspiratorial whisper.

"Thank you!" Maudie chuckled and headed out to the garden.

"Ah, Leanna, how lovely to see you again. This must be your sister, Jo. Pleased to meet you!"

"And you," Jo replied. "You must be Maudie."

Maudie nodded, and took a seat opposite them. "It's a pleasure to meet you. You live over in Braerannoch, aye? Leanna was saying you're a vet."

"Aye, I am. I'm doing my first placement at the moment.

78

I'm mainly in the clinic, but I'm moving onto livestock after that."

"There's trouble ahead, but it'll bring you all you hope for," Enid intoned, as the doorbell rang again and Paul arrived with Dougie.

"There you are!" Grace hissed. "I was wondering what was keeping you. Dinner is nearly ready!"

"We'll be right there," Paul called as the two men took off their dusty boots and washed their hands in the kitchen sink.

"We got held up with the ewes," Dougie said by way of explanation. "The dosing took all morning."

"Aye, well then, you've earned yourselves a well-earned break," Grace chided as she headed outside with the joint of beef and set it on the table. "Can you give me a hand with the vegetables?"

Dougie nodded, and soon the table was set with dishes of broccoli, green beans, carrots and peas as well as golden crispy roast potatoes, and a blue and white jug of gravy.

"Sit yourself down next to Jo," Grace told Dougie, pointing to the last empty chair, and he obediently sat down. Paul carved the beef and plated up as everyone sat down.

"I'd like to raise my glass to officially welcome Jo to Mossbrae, and to hope she has a lovely week, even though it was only meant to be the weekend."

"Slánte," said Jo, clinking her glass against hers. "Thank you for making me feel so welcome."

Since Eilidh and Angus had left the previous day, she and Leanna had had a lovely time exploring Mossbrae, a good distraction from recent events. They had gone to the Dog and Duck, and walked along the promenade, the beach and round the village. And for Jo it had felt like a home from home. She had even joined Grace and Paul on the farm, keeping an eye on the sheep, and she had prepared to be ready to head home today until they had found out the ferries were cancelled due to summer storms.

"Looks like you're stuck with me for the week!" she had laughed at the news.

"Och, you could see it as an extended holiday," Leanna replied. "You could take a tour of the farm and see the sheep. Are there any cattle farms near here, Robyn?"

"Aye, that'd be a grand idea," Robyn agreed. "There's a couple of farms we could go around."

"Thank you," Jo replied, feeling herself relax as they all started to eat.

"So, go on then," Leanna said as they drove back to Duck Cottage that evening. "Be honest, do you like Dougie? You two looked cosy sitting together earlier…"

"Leanna, I've only just split up from Colin," Jo said, looking uncomfortable.

"Och, I only meant as a friend… He seems nice and you two look like you get along. I think it's time you allowed yourself to be happy."

"I am happy," she replied, shaking her head as they drove up the drive toward Duck Cottage, and she did a double take as she took in the breathtaking view, with it's panoramic views of the beach and crashing waves beyond, the cottage sun kissed by late afternoon sunlight. It looked absolutely gorgeous. "*Och*! Look at that!"

"Aye, I cannae believe I get to live here either," Leanna grinned back as she let them in and they made their way to the back garden. "It used to be a holiday cottage, but Grace and

Paul are letting me rent here for the foreseeable future. If you're thinking of reasons to stay, this cottage would certainly be one of them, especially with the view from the back garden…"

Outside, the garden sloped downwards along the back wall, offering an even better view of the beach and crashing waves in all their glory. Jo nodded in agreement, as she sat down on the two seater bench. "I'm tempted to move in here myself so I could sit and admire that view all day."

"Fancy a wee dram out here whilst we sit and admire it?" Leanna suggested, sitting next to her. "The sunset is even more impressive."

"Aye, go on then," Jo said and Leanna went inside, returning with a bottle and two glasses, and two tartan blankets over her arm. "Here, so we can be cosy."

They sat together on the bench with their nest of blankets and cushions.

"Sláinte," Leanna said, clinking her glass against Jo's.

"Sláinte,"

"I think it's gonnae be a fun week," Leanna went on. "Especially as you'll get to know Dougie a wee bit better…"

"Och, Leanna… behave!" Jo chided gently.

"It'll be good to have a new friend. You were chatting away like a pair of finches at dinner. Everyone noticed. Especially The Trinity, and you know, they're excellent at matchmaking…"

"Ah, so that's why Grace was insistent that he sit next to me, and why The Trinity kept smiling at us!" Jo cried, laughing. "I've been set up!"

"Aye, but it's all good natured," Leanna replied. "They're harmless, and love nothing more than to see two people in love. Or, to see you smile and have something happy to smile about."

"Do they know about me and Colin?"

"Aye, they do. I might have mentioned it…"

Jo rolled her eyes good-naturedly. "*Leanna…*"

She took a sip of whisky and let out a long sigh. "I suppose you're right. I could do with something to smile about."

"Are you alright?" Leanna asked, putting an arm around her shoulders. "I thought you were coping ok with the split?"

"I honestly thought he was gonnae propose," Jo said quietly. "We'd been together for such a long time. Since school for goodness sake! And then, he just…left."

"Have you heard anything from him?" Leanna asked, but Jo shook her head. "Clean break and all that. His words, not mine."

"I'm so sorry. But think of it this way, maybe being here could be the right place to take your mind off things… A distraction. And, there's something more… Grace has given us enough honey cakes to stock our own bakery!"

Leanna produced Tupperware box from its hiding place under one of the blankets, and opened it. Jo took one with a smile, and took a sweet, delicious bite, mulling over Leanna's words, trying to ignore how much the whisky reminded her of the colour of Dougie's eyes.

A distraction was just what she needed.

Chapter Ten

How, exactly, did you get a sheep down from a shed roof?

Jo and Robyn exchanged glances as they arrived at Roddy Campbell's farm where he bred prize winning Scottish Blackface ewes. A few of Angus and Joe's flock were descended from one of Roddy's prize rams, and today, his daughter, Erin, had called them to help with Marigold, one of their pet ewes. A pet sheep was one of the names for an orphaned lamb who needed to be bottle fed, and hopefully adopted by another ewe.

Marigold peered down from the top of the lambing shed roof and bleated loudly, and Jo didn't know whether to laugh or cry.

"So what would you do?" Robyn asked, turning to her.

"We've tried tempting her down with food," Jo replied, ticking them off on her fingers. "We've tried calling her, and bribing her. Och, I'm gonnae have to climb up there and get her."

"I would do that too," Robyn agreed.

"We have to get her afore the storm hits," Jo added as she went and got a ladder, climbing up to the roof, where Marigold glared at her balefully for spoiling all the fun.

Sweating from the increasing heat of the late afternoon, Jo looked back at Marigold, like a mother whose toddler was testing her patience. At least this was Robyn's last call for the day and she and Leanna were heading to The Dog and Duck afterwards. She was going to need a stiff drink after this!

"Honestly, Marigold, how did you even get up here?" Jo asked Marigold, shaking her head.

"Erin said she was getting the ewes in, and Marigold decided she wanted to admire the view," Robyn called up.

"Something spooked her?"

"Not sure. I'm guessing so. But then again, she's always been a bit eccentric, according to Erin. She's a pet lamb. Erin's only here today because she's watching the farm for Roddy whilst he's away from the far for the day. She was hoping she would come down on her own by now… She's a stubborn one, is Marigold."

"Aye, you dinnae say," Jo muttered under her breath, trying to think of a plan, quick. "Right. I'm gonnae try and encourage her down. It should work as long as she doesnae leap off the other side of the roof!"

"Come on, Marigold. Good girl…" Jo said, stretching out a hand, but the ewe snorted and stamped her foot.

"I told you she was stubborn!" Robyn grinned, as Jo leant

forward, stretching out a hand, beckoning Marigold, who stood stock still.

"Aye, you can say that again!" Jo muttered. "Right, Marigold, if you willnae come to me, I'm coming to you..." Gingerly, she put one foot onto the roof and crept towards the ewe. "Marigold, you need to get off the roof now!"

Marigold grunted, and snorted, and took a step backwards as Jo crouched down, and crawled towards her.

"Come here, that's a good girl..." she called between gritted teeth. As much as she adored sheep, she'd never met one as stubborn as Marigold.

"Go on, Marigold," Robyn called, as Jo moved her hand in a slow shooing gesture, but Marigold stood her ground, and bleated in response.

Jo, who was now on all fours on the roof, edged towards Marigold, making gentle shooing movements to try and encourage her to move but Marigold remained where she was.

"Marigold, go back down. It's almost time for dinner!" Jo pleaded, glancing at Robyn, who started to chuckle.

"Dinnae laugh!" she pleaded. "It isnae funny."

"Come on now, Marigold, Jo is having a night out with Leanna tonight! She doesnae want to be late!" Robyn called up.

"Aye, that's right!" Jo added.

"And Dougie might be there."

"Will he?" Jo asked in surprise, turning around so quickly she nearly fell off the roof.

"Aye, he always has a night out on a Friday night," Robyn replied. "You two were getting on well the other day. He seems to like you..."

"Really?"

Her mind went back to his whisky coloured eyes and she felt her heart race a little bit faster. He liked her?

There was a bang of a car door, pulling Jo out of her thoughts. Jo and Marigold glanced over the side of the roof and gave an impatient bleat, to see Roddy Campbell had arrived back, and was staring up with barely concealed mirth.

"You look as if you need a hand…Come on now, Marigold!"

Then, without waiting for an answer, he gave a sharp, piercing whistle, and Marigold immediately turned around, and slowly made her way back down the side of the roof, leapt off, and rejoined the herd into the barn as though nothing out of the ordinary had happened.

"What the-" Jo cried, glancing from the ewe to Roddy, who started laughing uproariously.

"You're joking!" Robyn exclaimed as she burst out laughing at Jo's shocked face as she climbed down the ladder. She was still laughing as they reached the ground. "Have we missed something?"

"There's a simple explanation," Roddy explained when he had stopped laughing. "Wee Marigold thinks she's a goat. She loves to climb, and this is her latest party trick! She's done it every afternoon ever since she was a lamb…"

"And then he whistled, and she turned and leapt back off the roof!" Jo laughed, shaking her head as Leanna spluttered with laughter. "I cannae believe i climbed up on the roof for nothing! I was crawling along on all fours!"

Jo shook her head, heading to the bar to get the drinks. It was busy in The Dog and Duck tonight, as she waited to get served. She glanced across at their table where Leanna was still chuckling to herself.

"Crawling along a roof on all fours? Now that's an image," joked a voice behind her and she turned to see Dougie grinning at her. He was looked relaxed and happy, dressed in a pale blue t shirt, jeans and trainers, his dark hair dishevelled, and she was surprised to see he was freshly shaven.

His whisky coloured gaze met hers and despite herself she felt a jolt of attraction.

"Aye, it was something," Jo laughed. "Then Roddy arrived, whistled and she leapt straight down. Apparently, she thinks she's a goat."

"Och, I can just imagine...Jo vs Marigold! I've never met a sheep that thinks she's a goat. I'll have to look out next time we put them in the barn. You look nice. Can I get you got a drink? "

She was wearing a dark peacock blue dress, matching heels and feather earrings, red lipstick, and her dark auburn hair was worn loose around her shoulders.

"Thank you," she replied. "That's really kind but I was just going to get a bottle for me and Leanna. We're sitting over there."

"That's no problem. I'll get you both a drink," Dougie said easily as he waved Nigel over and ordered for them.

"There's a special on tonight," Leanna announced, waving the menu as Dougie and Jo headed back to the table with the drinks. "Lobster and fries. I overheard Nigel say he got a fresh seafood order in this morning."

"That has my name on it. I might get some myself." Dougie grinned, and Jo nodded in agreement.

"Why don't you join us?" Leanna asked, smiling at Jo. "I'll go and order the food."

Leanna went to the bar to order, and Dougie slid into the booth opposite her.

"So how was your day when you weren't climbing shed roofs?" He asked as he sipped his beer.

"It was fun," Jo replied, sipping her wine. "We went to a few cattle farms and it was good to get some experience with cattle. How have things been at Cairnmhor?"

"The usual, checking the ewes and the deer. They're gearing up for the rut soon. It's spectacular to watch. You can already hear the stags roaring. It's an eerie, haunting sound. You'll have to come and hear it next time you're back in Mossbrae."

"I will," Jo replied, enthusiastically.

"Och, I'm gonnae miss it when I leave," Dougie added, sadly, taking a sip of his beer.

"You're leaving?" She blurted and to her own surprise, she felt a pang of sadness and disappointment. "When? Why?"

"Aye, I head home every winter to help my Da. He's in the thick of lambing season in early winter and he cannae do it all alone."

"But you'll be back in Mossbrae in the spring?"

Dougie nodded. "Aye, Angus and Eilidh need me here, and to be honest, I'm really starting to fall in love with Mossbrae. It's a lovely little village and I'm coming to think of it as home. How about you? You'll be heading back to Braerannoch when the storms abaits, aye?"

Jo nodded. "I've got my placement, but I can come back at weekends. I've told Leanna I'd make more of an effort to visit more often."

Dougie met her gaze and nodded, his eyes suddenly serious. "It would be good to see you again before I go."

Jo smiled back at him. "You've been really kind to me whilst I've been here. I feel like I'm in a home from home."

Dougie smiled back, and Jo was peaked with sudden curiosity as to what it would be like to kiss him. That thought made her blush.

"Am I interrupting?" Leanna asked brightly as she returned.

Dougie hesitated, and Jo could feel his gaze on her as he finished his beer. "I should get going. It's been lovely to see you again. Catch you again afore you go?"

Jo nodded. "I'm gonnae call at Cairnmhor to check the ewes tomorrow. Robyn isnae able to have so much contact with the sheep now."

"Because of the baby, aye," Dougie agreed. He stood and gave her a wave. "I'll see you tomorrow then."

"Arranging a date?" Leanna joked, as she slid into the seat next to her sister.

"No. It isnae a date!" Jo replied, flushing.

But why did it feel like one, she thought with sudden giddiness at the thought of seeing him again.

Chapter Eleven

*T*he following morning was bright and fresh, and Jo woke early, filled with excitement that she was heading to Cairnmhor, and that she was going to see Dougie again. Despite telling herself she wasn't going to jump into another relationship, she couldn't stop thinking about him, or his gorgeous whisky coloured eyes.

Her phone pinged, and she glanced down to see Leanna had added a new post to her Instagram page. Automatically, Jo liked it, and scrolled through her own page. Then, she saw it, Colin's Instagram page, and her curiosity was peaked. From his profile photo, he looked exactly the same as he had done the last time she had seen him three months ago, the same blond hair, grey-blue eyes and slightly crooked nose where he'd been kicked by a horse as a child. If anything, she thought, feeling a rush of confused mixed emotions, he looked even better. He was wearing a grey and blue striped beanie, and ski jacket, and she remembered it was almost Christmas in New Zealand.

Then, Jo saw her, and her heart sank.

Colin had his arm around a pretty brunette wearing a pink

striped bobble hat. She had her hand outstretched, and Jo saw the diamond solitaire engagement ring, and when she read the caption, she felt like she'd been stabbed in the heart:

She said yes!!

"Are you alright?" Leanna asked, through a mouthful of toast. "You look like you've seen a ghost."

"I sort of have?" Jo replied, showing her Colin's Instagram page.

"Och! Jings! I'm so sorry!" she cried, pulling her into a tight hug. "Are you alright?"

"No," Jo replied, feeling her throat tighten with emotion. "We were together for such a long time, and then he meets someone three months later... I feel like I wasnae good enough."

"Och, it wasnae that!" Leanna cried. "You know that. I'm so sorry..."

She took her in her arms and held her tightly. "And I'm sorry you found out like this though. Could his sister no' have called you? Broken the news gently?"

"No." Jo asked. "We've lost touch since I came here, and anyway, despite dating her brother for almost a decade, we were never that close."

She exhaled slowly and grabbed her car keys, wiping her eyes, determined not to let her past ruin her day. "I have to get over to Cairnmhor. I'll see you later."

Dougie was already waiting for her at the farmhouse when she arrived.

"Morning," he said amiably as she parked up and got out. "Ready to see the sheep?"

"Where is everyone?"

"Grace has taken the kids to school, and Paul is out with Joe at the suppliers."

"Aye, let's go. Shall we take the quad?" Dougie asked, gesturing to the quad bike, and handing her a helmet.

"Thanks. Are you driving or shall I?"

"You can drive a quad bike?"

"Aye. I grew up on a farm to remember? I've been riding quad bikes since I was a toddler."

Dougie face cracked into a grin. "Come on then, let's go. You can drive."

They put their helmets on and climbed onto the quad bike and Jo tried to ignore the thrill of Dougie's arms around her waist as she started the engine.

They rode up the hillside to where the ewes were scattered around the moor.

"They look healthy from here," Jo said, admiring the ewes. "They're in good condition. I can see that from here."

"Aye. They're good stock," Dougie replied with a nod. "Angus buys them from auction from Roddy Campbell's stock. He's got some grand pedigree lines."

"Do you think they'll be another Marigold in next year's lambs?" Jo giggled.

Dougie shrugged. "I hope so. She sounds a lot of fun!"

They turned to each other, grinning.

Jo looked up and her gaze met his, and for a moment, she was drowning in his eyes.

"Shall we check on the deer whilst we're here?" He suggested and she nodded, and they walked over towards the deer paddock.

"I meant it, you know," he said after a pause as they admired the deer.

"What?" Jo asked.

"Come back during the rut and see the deer. I'd like that."

Jo couldn't help but smile back. "I'd like that too."

"Are you alright?"

Jo hesitated but something in his gaze told her she could tell him and he wouldn't judge her. "Actually, I'm not... I just found out my ex got engaged."

"Jings," Dougie murmured. "I'm sorry. Are you alright?"

"It's not that I'm not over him," Jo replied quickly. "I'm healing from that, and you've helped me so much, our friendship, I mean... but it's the fact he and I were together so long, but he didn't even mention marriage..."

"He's a fool," Dougie replied. "If I was with you, I'd have a proposed in a heartbeat."

"Really?" Jo asked, glancing at him, expecting him to laugh but when he didn't, she felt the butterflies of desire in the pit of her stomach.

"Of course. You're wonderful..."

"Thank you."

He met her gaze, and for a second, and for a moment, she thought he was going to say more when she spotted something out of the corner of her eye.

"Oh Jings! Fire!"

The stubble had caught alight in the summer heat and now, smoke was billowing into the air.

"Take the quad back to the farmhouse and get Paul and Grace!" Dougie shouted, running down the hill back towards the deer paddock without hesitation.

"Alright," Jo didn't need telling twice. She ran to the quad bike, and drove it back down the hill to the farmhouse.

"Jo? Is everything alright?" Grace asked, rushing out at the sound of the quad bike.

"There's a fire up on the hillside neat the deer paddock. Some of the stubble caught light."

"I'll call the fire brigade," Grace replied without hesitation. "Where's Dougie?"

"He's up there still, trying to deal with the deer."

"Once I've called the fire brigade, head back up to the top of the hill. There's a footpath leading up to the top of the hill which leads to the main road, and the fire engine can get to you easier."

Jo nodded, reaching for her mobile and called Dougie, checking he was alright.

"I'll head back up and give Dougie a hand moving the deer," she told Grace, and climbed back onto the quad, speeding away.

Once she reached the brow of the hill, she could see the fire was spreading. Dougie was trying to move the deer.

"Are you alright?" She called. "I've let Grace know! She said that once we get the deer to safety, we need to stand near the road to await the fire brigade."

"It's alright, I'm coping!" He called back as he went into the deer paddock to move the deer. "I dinnae think we need to move them out of the paddock, but we need to get them as far away from the fire as possible."

He gently spread his arms and walked towards the deer,

who instinctively moved away, heading to the other side of the paddock. "Can you head up to the top of the hill to wait for the fire brigade? I can handle the deer. They're more familiar with me and it might be easier for me to move them."

Jo nodded, understanding as she took the quad and waited for the fire brigade. She glanced down at the field now, watching the smoke pluming from where the stubble had set alight. It was spreading fast and she hoped the fire engine would be here soon.

The road at the top of the hill was quiet and it was an anxious wait. From here, Jo could see the deer paddock, the burning stubble, and in the far distance the farmhouse. She felt a surge of fear grip here, not wanting to have to call Eilidh and tell her things had gone wrong.

Then to her relief, there was the wail of a siren.

"This way!" She called as the fire engine arrived and she lead them down the hill towards the fire. It was quickly spreading towards the deer paddock but soon, the fire was put out, and Jo breathed a sigh of relief as she called Grace and let her know the fire was out, and everyone was safe.

"We did it!" Jo cried in delight, flinging her arms around Dougie's neck. He looked down at her and their gaze met for a long moment, and Jo felt her cheeks flame with sudden shyness. Then, before she could stop herself, she reached up and kissed him.

It was a soft, shy kiss but as she pulled away, she could feel her lips burning with desire.

"I'm sorry," she stammered, staring into his eyes. "I, um, dinnae know why I did that..."

"I'm no' complaining," Dougie replied, his face cracking

into a grin. Jo became aware that he was still holding her in his arms, as he pulled her towards him and kissed her again until her head spun.

Suddenly, Jo's phone sprang into life, making them leap apart as she answered it, voice shaking. "Hello?"

"I've got some more good news!" Grace came brightly down the line. "The ferries are running again. The ash cloud has moved south, away from Paris. I'm gonnae go and give Angus and Eilidh a call. Maybe they could head to Paris after all!"

Chapter Twelve

raerannoch

"Thank you for having us," Eilidh said, hugging Alice tightly as she and Angus waited for the ferry back to Mossbrae. "It's been a lovely week, even with the storm causing chaos!"

"Aye, we cannae thank you enough for all your help," Alice replied. "I'm so glad you've had a wonderful time. Come back soon, won't you?"

"We'll come to see you with the Valais Blacknose ewes," Ray cut in.

"Och, that's so kind of you," Angus replied as the ferry approached the harbour.

"Have a safe trip. We'll see you soon!" Alice called as they got back in the car and drove down the ramp onto the ferry.

"See you soon!"

∼

"I cannae believe we're heading home," Eilidh sighed as she watched the waves gently lapping against the beach as the ferry headed away from the harbour.

"Aye, it's been an interesting week!" Angus replied, squeezing her hand. "But we've had a grand honeymoon, aye?"

"It's been a memorable one!" she exclaimed as Angus's phone beeped and he saw there was a voicemail from Grace.

"Och, well that is good news," he announced after he had listening to it, his face cracking into a grin. "Grace said the ash cloud has moved from over Europe, it's moving and the flights to Europe are outgoing again."

"Really?" Eilidh asked. "What does that mean for us?"

"Well, if you wanted to go on honeymoon to Paris, we could? To have the honeymoon we originally planned?"

He stepped towards her and took her in his arms. "What do you think? Grace suggested we book a flight and we could go this weekend if you'd like to?"

Eilidh thought about it for a moment, looking up at him. "I've really enjoyed our honeymoon, it's been wonderful. We've been able to spend time together which is all I want-ed." She shook her head. "I dinnae think we need to go to Paris for a 'proper' honeymoon. We could maybe go for our wedding anniversary next year?"

"Aye, that's a grand idea, if you want to do that." He bent his head and kissed her. "All I want is for you to be happy."

"I am happy, wherever we are," Eilidh replied, smiling up at him. "I've had a lovely time here, despite the weather. It's felt like a home from home."

"We could even come back here again, if you want to," Angus suggested. "Have another holiday, maybe stay for a couple of weeks…"

"Aye, that sounds wonderful…"

A few hours later, they reached Mossbrae, and drove home to Honeybee Cottage.

"You're back!" Grace cried, rushing towards them joyfully. "How was your honeymoon?"

"Wonderful, apart from the storm causing a bit of chaos! Braerannoch is a wonderful place to stay. We're gonnae stay there again in the future." Eilidh replied. "How have things been here?"

"We looked after the bees whilst you were gone!" Mhairi piped up excitedly. "They've been really good, and well behaved, and were taking plenty of pollen from the ivy!"

"That's wonderful, I'm so glad! Thank you so much for looking after them for me." Eilidh cried, pulling them both into a tight hug. "I missed you both so much."

"Did you get my voicemail?" Grace asked. "Are you gonnae go to Paris now the ash cloud has passed?"

"We're thinking of going for our anniversary," Angus replied, putting an arm around Eilidh's shoulders.

"So, any honeymoon babies?"

"No, not yet," Eilidh chuckled, exchanging a look with Angus. "Maybe in the future. I'm waiting for my niece or nephew's arrival…"

She turned to Robyn now, admiring how she was glowing with happiness. She looked wonderful.

"You look wonderful!" she called over. "How have you been?"

"Och, you've only been gone for a week!" Robyn said with a soft chuckle. "I'm fine. Baby is fine. Jo's done a grand job, helping me keep an eye on the livestock whilst you were gone. They're all fine, and Jo and Dougie has done a braw job."

"Thank you both so much," Angus said, turning to Jo and Dougie now.

"Och, it was all Dougie," Jo replied, turning to him now. "Especially with the fire."

"What fire?" Angus exclaimed. "You didnae mention a fire!"

"The stubble caught fire but the fire brigade got here in time."

"The deer were safe," Dougie added. "Jo and I moved them to the far end of the paddock and they were well away from the fire."

Angus blew air through his teeth. "Jings! Well, I'm glad you're both here. Thank you. We should celebrate tonight, let's all go to the Dog and Duck."

"That's a grand idea," Grace replied.

"Och, it's grand to have you back," said Maudie as she sipped her sherry.

"Home is where the heart is," End intoned. "We all need to look to the future now."

"Quite right," Eilidh replied as she sipped her own drink, glancing across at Dougie and Jo who were deep in conversation at the bar.

"Speaking of the future, those two look cosy..." Eilidh said conspiratorially.

"Aye, I think we have a new romance budding on the horizon," said Maudie delightedly. "They've been getting on like a pair of lovebirds whilst you were away."

"That's promising."

"So you're heading home tomorrow," Dougie said, sipping his drink.

Jo nodded. "Aye, back to Braerannoch. But I'll be back in October, to see the rut."

"Aye, I'll look forward to seeing you. If I dinnae see you afore that. I might come and see you in Braerannoch."

"Aye, I'd like that."

Jo tucked a stray hair behind her ear. "Listen, Dougie, can we talk, about yesterday? About our kiss…"

"I've been thinking about that too," Dougie replied, leaning towards her. "I really like you, Jo…"

"That's the thing, Dougie. I really like you. But I'm sorry, I'd like to take it slowly, stay friends for now… Especially with you leaving for the winter, and me heading back to Braerannoch…"

"That's fine for me," Dougie replied, his gaze met her's, his whisky coloured gaze boring down on her. "I'm happy with us being friends…For now…"

Jo met his gaze, and couldn't help but smile.

"They'll be another wedding soon, I bet," Leanna replied, with a mischievous grin.

"I dinnae think we'll have to wait too long. I think she and Dougie would make a great couple," Maudie sighed happily.

"A grand matchmaking plan."

Eilidh nodded excitedly. "We need to get our hats ready."

"Och, I cannae wait for the future," Robyn exclaimed, smiling. "A new baby… A new love story…"

"Aye," Eilidh added, putting an arm around her shoulders, her heart singing with happiness as she caught Angus grinning at her from across the table. "A lot to look forward too!"

THE END

Other Works

Thank you so much for choosing this book. I hope you enjoyed it.

This series is a standalone series so can be read in any order.

If you would like to read the books from the beginning, to when Angus and Eilidh first met, here is the series in chronological order:

1. A Year at Honeybee Cottage

2. Christmas at Honeybee Cottage (A Mossbrae Short Story)

3. A Summer Wedding in the Highlands

4. A Honeymoon at Seaside Cottage.

Acknowledgements

Firstly, a big thank you to my family and friends for all their support publishing this, my fourth(!) book. Finally, the finished product is here for you all to enjoy.

Secondly, I'd like to give a special thank you to Kirsty, for the fantastic manuscript appraisal. You know exactly what I'm trying to say and how to make it even better.

Finally, as always, this book wouldn't be the same without the detailed research about beekeeping which is the foundation of this series. I wouldn't be able to do this with the wonderful Youtube videos from Gwenyn Gruffyd. Your videos are invaluable!

Lots of love.

Alexandra.

About The Author

Hello! Thank you so much for picking my book. I hope you enjoy it as much as I enjoyed writing it!

Here's a little bit about me:

I am a full time indie romance author of my Scottish contemporary romance series, set in the fictional Scottish village of Mossbrae.

Originally from Yorkshire, I was brought up in a multicultural household (Scottish, British, and Hong Kong Chinese.) I now live in the East Midlands with my husband and two children.

Having always dreamt of being an author, and after a long journey of twenty years, in June 2022, I published my debut novel, A Year at Honeybee Cottage.

I now write full time, but when I'm not, I enjoy knitting (toy animals, using Claire Garland's brilliant knitting patterns,) exploring National Trust places with my family on weekends, and binge watching tv boxsets.

I am currently watching Chinese dramas (Till the End of the Moon and My Journey to You) as research for my next book: my debut Chinese inspired fantasy romance, which is out next year.

Get in touch with me on my updated writer's contacts on:
Instagram @alexwholeywriter
Threads @alexwholeywriter@threads.net
Love Alexandra. X

Printed in Great Britain
by Amazon

35793343R00071